BELLAROO CREEK

**Three brave women, three strong men...
and one town on the brink**

Bellaroo Creek in the Australian Outback
is a town in need of rescue! So the arrival of
three single women and a few adorable kids
is exactly the injection of life it needs. Are
the town and its ruggedly gorgeous cattlemen
prepared for the adventure ahead?

One town, three heart-warming romances
to cherish forever!

THE CATTLEMAN'S READY-MADE FAMILY
by Michelle Douglas
in July 2013

MIRACLE IN BELLAROO CREEK
by Barbara Hannay
in August 2013

PATCHWORK FAMILY IN THE OUTBACK
by Soraya Lane
in September 2013

Dear Reader,

Writing can be a very solitary business. I love what I do, but sometimes I miss the human contact of a regular job! This book was unique to write, though, because the town of Bellaroo Creek was devised not just by me, but by two other wonderful authors.

This is the third book in the *Bellaroo Creek* series, about a town that is in desperate need of new residents. Many small towns in rural Australia struggle with their population, which has led to some innovative ideas to breathe fresh life into communities.

Bellaroo Creek is a town that all the locals are passionate about saving, but in the end everything hinges on finding a sole charge teacher for the local primary school. In this book you'll meet heroine Poppy Carter— a young woman who leaves the city to start afresh in rural Australia.

Poppy has had her share of heartbreak, which is why she does everything in her power to stay clear of sexy single dad Harrison Black. Little does she know that Harrison is as determined to stay alone as she is...only things don't always go to plan.

I hope you enjoy this story and, if you've read the two books in the series before it, enjoy being back in Bellaroo Creek as well!

If you'd like to know more about me or my books visit my website: www.sorayalane.com

Soraya

PATCHWORK FAMILY IN THE OUTBACK

BY
SORAYA LANE

First published in Great Britain 2013
by Mills & Boon, an imprint of Harlequin (UK) Limited.
Harlequin (UK) Limited, Eton House, 18-24 Paradise Road,
Richmond, Surrey TW9 1SR

© Soraya Lane 2013

ISBN: 978 0 263 23547 0

Harlequin (UK) policy is to use papers that are natural, renewable
and recyclable products and made from wood grown in sustainable
forests. The logging and manufacturing process conform to the
legal environmental regulations of the country of origin.

Writing for Mills & Boon® is truly a dream come true for **Soraya Lane**. An avid reader and writer since her childhood, Soraya describes becoming a published author as 'the best job in the world' and hopes to be writing heart-warming, emotional romances for many years to come.

Soraya lives with her own real-life hero on a small farm in New Zealand, surrounded by animals and with an office overlooking a field where their horses graze.

For more information about Soraya and her upcoming releases visit her at her website, www.sorayalane.com, her blog, www.sorayalane.blogspot.com, or follow her at www.facebook.com/SorayaLaneAuthor

Recent books by Soraya Lane:

MISSION: SOLDIER TO DADDY
THE SOLDIER'S SWEETHEART
THE NAVY SEAL'S BRIDE
BACK IN THE SOLDIER'S ARMS
RODEO DADDY
THE ARMY RANGER'S RETURN
SOLDIER ON HER DOORSTEP

**Did you know these are also available as eBooks?
Visit www.millsandboon.co.uk**

This book is dedicated to my incredible support crew... My mother, Maureen, because I wouldn't be able to write one book without you helping me with the 'little emperor' on a daily basis, and Natalie and Nicola for our fabulous emails and chats. I'm so lucky to have you all in my corner.

ARE YOU OUR NEW TEACHER?

- *Do you love children and like the idea of running a small country school?*
- *Do you want a fresh start in a welcoming rural town?*
- *Do you want to be a cherished part of our community?*

Then come visit us in Bellaroo Creek! If you're a dedicated teacher capable of running our small school, then we'd love to meet you. Rent a home for only $1 a week and help to save our school and *our town.*

CHAPTER ONE

POPPY CARTER STOOD in the center of her new classroom and clasped her hands behind her back to stop them from shaking. Had she taken on more than she could handle?

The desks were lined against the walls with chairs stacked on top of them, and the floor was clean and tidy, but it was the walls that were sending shivers down her spine. Where was the fun? Where were the bright colors that should adorn the room to welcome young pupils?

She sighed and walked to the main desk, pulling out the chair and sinking into it. Her problem was that she'd always been at schools with a half-decent budget, and she knew that this school was barely able to keep the doors open, let alone redecorate.

Poppy dropped her forehead to the desktop before resting her cheek against it instead and staring at the wall. She had a lot to do before tomorrow, and there was no way she was going to start her class in a room like this.

New beginnings, a fresh start and a bright future.

That's why she'd come here, and she was determined to make that happen.

"Hello?"

Poppy sat bolt upright. Either she was hearing things in this spooky old room or there was someone else here.

"Hello?"

The deep male voice was closer this time. Before she could call back, it was followed by a body. One that filled the entire doorway.

"Hi," she said, glancing toward the closest window, planning her escape route in case she needed one.

"I didn't mean to disturb you." The man smiled at her, one side of his mouth turning up as he nudged the tip of his hat and leaned into the room. "We've had a bit of trouble here lately and I wanted to make sure there weren't any kids up to no good."

Poppy swallowed and nodded. "I'm probably not meant to be here myself, but I wanted to have a good look around and see if there was anything that needed doing."

Chocolate-brown eyes met hers, softer than before, and matched with a dimple when the man finally gave her a full smile. "I take it you're the famous Ms. Carter, then?"

Poppy couldn't help grinning back. "Take out the famous part and call me Poppy, and I'd say that's me."

He chuckled, removed his hat and stepped forward, hand extended. There was a gruffness about him that she guessed came with the territory of being a rancher, but up close he was even more handsome than he'd been from a distance. Strong, wide shoulders, a jaw that looked as if it had been carved from stone and the deepest dark brown eyes she'd ever seen....

Poppy cleared her throat and clasped his hand.

"Harrison Black," he said, hand firm against hers. "My kids go to school here."

Right. So he was married with children. It didn't explain his lack of a wedding band, but then plenty of ranchers probably never wore a ring, especially when they were working. But it did make her feel less nervous about being in the room with him.

"How many children do you have?" she asked.

The smile was back at the mention of his children. "Two. Kate and Alex. They're out there in the truck."

Poppy looked out the window, spotting his vehicle. "I'm just heading back to my place for some supplies, so how about I say hi to them?"

He shrugged, put his hat on his head and took a couple of steps backward. The heels of his boots were loud on the wooden floor, making her look up again. And when she did she wished she hadn't, because *his* eyes had never left hers and a frown was hovering at the corners of his mouth.

Instead of acknowledging him she reached for her bag and slung it over her shoulder, and when she looked back he was already halfway to the door.

"Ms. Carter, what made you come here?"

She met his gaze, chin held high, not wanting to answer the man standing in front of her, but knowing it was a question she'd be asked countless times from the moment she started meeting locals—as soon as her pupils began flooding through the door, parents anxiously following them.

"I needed a change," she told him honestly, even if she was omitting a large part of the truth. "When I saw the advertisements for Bellaroo, I figured it was time for me to take a chance."

Harrison was still staring at her, but she broke the contact. Walked past him and down the short hall to the front door.

"And a new haircut or color wasn't enough of a change?"

She spun on the spot, temper flaring. This man, this *Harrison*, didn't know the first thing about her, but to suggest a haircut? Did she look like some floozy who just needed a new lipstick to make her problems go away?

"No," she said, glaring at him, feet rooted to the spot. "I wanted to make a difference, and keeping this school open seemed pretty important to your community, unless I've been mistaken?"

His eyes gave away nothing, his broad shoulders squared and his body grew rigid. "There's nothing more important to me than this school staying open. But if you don't work out? If we've taken a chance on the wrong person? Then we don't just lose a school, we'll lose our entire town." He sighed. "Forgive me if I don't think you look like a woman who could go a week without hitting the shops or beauty salon."

She let him pull the door shut and marched toward his vehicle, desperate to see his children. Right now they were the only things that could cool her down, and the last thing she wanted was to get into an argument with a rude, arrogant man who had no idea what kind of person she was or what she believed in. To even suggest... She swallowed and took a deep breath.

"I think you'll find I know exactly how much this school means to Bellaroo Creek," she said over her shoulder, in a voice as calm as she could manage. "And please don't pretend you know me or anything about me. Do I make myself clear?"

She could have sworn a hint of a smile flashed across Harrison's face, but she was too angry to care.

"Crystal clear," he said, striding past her.

If she hadn't known two little children were watching them from the truck, she would have poked her tongue out. But Poppy just kept walking, and sent up a silent prayer that she'd never have to talk to their father ever again.

Harrison knew he'd behaved badly. But honestly? He didn't care. Speaking his mind to the teacher hadn't exactly been his best move, but if she didn't hang around, then their town was done for. He'd needed to say it now because if she changed her mind they'd have to find someone else *fast*. The future of Bellaroo Creek meant more to him than anything. Because otherwise he'd lose everything he'd ever worked for, just to keep his children close.

He swung open the passenger door. "Kids, this is your new teacher."

They looked out—all angelic blond hair and blue

eyes. A constant reminder of their mother, and probably the only reason he didn't still hate the woman.

"I'm Ms. Carter." Harrison listened to the new teacher introduce herself, watching the anger disappear from her face as soon as she locked eyes on his children. "Your dad found me in the middle of planning your classroom."

"Planning?" he asked.

She smiled and leaned against the open door, but he had a feeling her happy expression was for his children's benefit, not his. "I can't teach young children in a room that looks like the inside of a hospital," she told him. "I don't have long, but in the morning it'll look deserving of kids."

"You're making it look better?"

Harrison grinned as his daughter spoke. She played the shy card for all of a minute with strangers, then couldn't keep herself from talking.

"I want us to have fun, and that means putting a smile on your face from the second you walk through my door in the morning."

So maybe she wasn't so bad, but it wasn't exactly evidence that the teacher would hang around for the long haul. He'd had enough experience to know that an isolated rural town wasn't exactly paradise for everyone, especially for a teacher expected to teach children of all ages.

"If you need a hand…" he found himself saying.

She smiled politely at him, but he could see the storm still brewing in her eyes. "Thank you, Mr. Black, but I'm sure I can manage."

He stared at her long and hard before walking around to the driver's side. "I'll look forward to seeing in the morning what you've done with the place."

The teacher shut the passenger door and leaned in the window. "Your wife won't be dropping the children off?"

Harrison gave her a cool smile. "No, it'll be me."

He watched as she straightened, a question crossing her face even though she never said anything.

"I'll see you kids tomorrow," she called out, walking backward.

Harrison touched his hat and pulled out into the road, glancing in the rearview mirror to see her standing there still, one hand holding her long hair back from her face, the other shielding her eyes from the sun.

She was pretty, he'd give her that, but there was no way she was going to stick it out here as their teacher. He could tell just from looking at her. And that meant he had to figure out what the hell he was going to do if she left. Because staying in Bellaroo wasn't going to be an option for him if the school closed down, nor any of the other families who loved this town as much as he did.

"Daddy, don't you think we should help our teacher?"

Harrison sighed and glanced back at his daughter. "I think she'll be fine, Katie," he told her.

She sighed in turn. "It's a pretty big classroom."

Harrison stared straight ahead. The last thing he needed was to grow a conscience when it came to their new teacher, and he had errands to run for the rest of the afternoon. But maybe his daughter had a point. If he didn't want her to up and leave, then maybe he needed to make more of an effort. They all did.

"We might go back later on and see what we can do. How does that sound?"

"Great!" Katie was elbowing her brother, as if they'd both somehow managed to pull the wool over his eyes. "We could take her dinner and help her do the walls."

Harrison stayed silent. Helping Ms. Carter redecorate? Maybe. Taking her dinner? *Hell, no.*

CHAPTER TWO

HARRISON LIKED TO think of himself as a strong man. He worked the land, could hunt and keep his family alive and comfortable in the wilderness if he had to, and yet his seven-year-old daughter managed to wrangle him as if he were a newborn calf.

"Dad, I think she'll like this."

He stared at his pint-size kid and tried to look fierce. "I am *not* buying a cake to take her."

Katie wrapped one arm around his leg and put her cheek against his jean-clad thigh. "But Daddy, it wouldn't be a picnic without a cake."

"It's not a picnic," he told her, "so there's no problem."

His daughter giggled. "Well, it is, kind of."

He looked at the cake. It did look good and they were being sold for charity, but what kind of message would that be sending if he arrived to help with *cake*? Taking sausages, bread and ketchup was one thing, because he could let the kids help their new teacher while he used the barbecue out back. But this was going too far.

"Daddy?"

He tried to ignore the blue eyes looking up at him, pleading with him. And failed. "Okay, we'll take the cake. But don't go thinking we'll be spending all night there. It's just something to eat, some quick help and then home. Okay?"

Katie smiled and he couldn't help but do the same back. His little girl sure knew how to wrap him around her finger. "Come on, Alex," Harrison called.

His son appeared from behind an aisle and they finally reached the cashier. Harrison had known old Mrs. Jones since he was a boy and was still buying his groceries from her and her husband.

"So what are you all doing in town today?"

He started to place items on the counter. "Had a few errands to run, so we're a bit out of sequence."

"And now we're going to see our new teacher," announced Katie.

"So you've already met Ms. Carter?"

Harrison frowned. He didn't like everyone knowing his business, even if he did live in a small town with a gossip mill that ignited at any hint of something juicy. "We're going to help her make some changes to the classroom, aren't we, kids?"

Katie and Alex nodded as he paid for the groceries and hauled the bags from the counter.

"It's mighty nice to have someone like Poppy Carter in town. Like a ray of sunshine when she came in this morning, she was."

He smiled politely back. He didn't need to feel any worse about how he'd spoken to her earlier, because no matter how much he tried to think otherwise, he did care that he'd been rude. It wasn't his nature, and he realized now it might have been uncalled for. Did he doubt that she'd stick it out? Sure. But maybe he should have been more encouraging, rather than sending her scurrying back to wherever she'd come from before she'd even started.

"So what do you think?"

Harrison looked up and squinted at Mrs. Jones. He had no idea what she'd just asked him. "Sorry?"

"About whether she has a husband? Suzie Croft met her and was certain she had a mark on her finger where a ring had been, but I told her it was none of our business why she'd come here without a husband." The older woman tut-tutted. "We advertised for someone looking for a fresh start, and that's what we can give her. Isn't that right?"

Harrison raised an eyebrow. Mrs. Jones liked to gossip better than all the rest of them combined. "I'd say we'll just have to wait to find out more about Ms. Carter, once she's good and ready to tell us her business."

Who cared if she was married or not? Or whether she had a husband. All he cared about was that she was kind to his children, taught them well and stuck around to keep the school from closure. Tick all three off the list and he wouldn't care if she was married to a darn monkey.

"Thanks," he called over his shoulder as he carried the groceries out the door. "See you later in the week."

The little bell above tinkled when he pushed the

door open. He waited for his kids to catch up and race past him.

An hour at the school, then back home—that was the plan. And he was darned if he wasn't going to stick to it.

Poppy was starting to think she'd taken on more than she could cope with. The room was looking like a complete bomb site, and she didn't know where to start. It wasn't as if she could just pop down to a paint store and buy some bright colors to splash on the walls. Here it was do it yourself or don't do it at all.

She sighed and gathered her hair up into a high ponytail, sick of pushing it off her face each time she bent down.

Right now she had a heap of bright orange stars she'd cut out from a stack of paper, ready to stick together and pin across one wall. Then she planned on decorating one rumpty old wall with huge hearts and stars made with her silver sprinkles, before drawing the outline of a large tree for the older children to color in for her. She had stickers of animals and birds that could be placed on the branches, but for everything else she was going to have to rely on her own artistic skills. And her own money.

She didn't have as much of that as she was used to, but at least being here meant she didn't have anywhere to spend it. Groceries from the local store, her measly one-dollar rent and enough to keep the house running—it was all she needed, and she was going to make it work.

"Hello?"

Poppy jumped. Either she was starting to hear things or she wasn't alone. Again. But surely it wasn't...

Harrison Black. Only this time he brought his children with him into the room.

"Hey," she said, standing up and stretching her back. "What are you guys doing here?"

Harrison held up two bags, a smile kicking up the corners of his mouth. "We come bearing gifts," he said.

She grinned at the children as they stood close to their dad, both smiling at her. So this was his way of apologizing—coming back with something to bribe her with.

"You're not here to help me, are you?" she asked them, crouching down, knowing they'd approach her if she was at their level.

It worked. Both children came closer, shuffling in her direction.

"Now, let me try to remember," she said, looking from one child to the other. "You're Alex—" she pointed to the girl "—and you're Katie, right?"

They both burst out laughing, shaking their heads.

"No!" Katie giggled. "*I'm* Katie and *he's* Alex."

Poppy laughed along with them before glancing up at their dad. "I'm glad that's sorted then. Imagine if I'd got that wrong tomorrow?"

The children started to inspect her bits and pieces, so she moved closer to Harrison. She wasn't one to hold grudges, and with two happy children in the room, it wasn't exactly easy not to smile in his direction. Even if he had been beyond rude less than a few hours earlier.

"So what's in the bag?" she asked him.

"A peace offering," he replied, one hand braced against the door as he watched her.

Poppy just raised her eyebrows, waiting for him to continue.

"Dinner for us all."

Her eyebrows rose even farther at that. "Your idea or theirs?" she asked, hooking a finger in the kids' direction.

Harrison sighed, and it made her smile. She guessed he wasn't used to apologies or to being questioned. "Theirs, but it was a good one, if that makes it sound any better."

Poppy was done with grilling him. "I'm just kidding. It's the thought that counts, and I'm starving."

He held up the paper bags and cringed. "I just had a really bad thought—that you might be vegetarian."

She shook her head. "I'd like to be, but I'm not." Poppy took the bags from him and placed them on an upturned desk. "I love that they still use paper bags here."

"Plastic is the devil, according to Mrs. Jones, so don't even get her *started* on that topic." Harrison stood back, letting Poppy inspect the contents. "Although she has an opinion about most things, so that kind of applies for any questions you throw her way."

Poppy laughed and pulled out the cake. "Now, this is what I call a peace offering!"

A hand on her leg made her turn.

"The cake was my idea." Katie pointed at it. "Daddy said no, but…"

"Uh-hmm." Harrison cleared his throat, placing a

hand on his daughter's shoulder. "How about you help Ms. Carter and I'll head out and fire up the barbecue?"

Poppy grinned and let Katie take her hand and lead her back to the pile of things she'd been working on.

Harrison Black might be gruff and forthright, but his daughter had him all figured out.

Poppy looked over her shoulder as he walked out the door, bag under one arm as he strode off to cook dinner. His shoulders were broad, once again nearly filling the doorway as he passed through. And she was certain that he'd be wondering why the hell he'd let his daughter talk him into coming back to help her.

Harrison was starting to realize he hadn't planned this at all. They had no napkins, no plates and an old pair of tongs was his only usable utensil. His one saving grace was that the ketchup was in a squeeze bottle.

He looked up to see his children running toward him. It was still light, but that was fading, the day finally cooling off. He usually loved this time, when he came in for the day and settled down with his kids. And he was thinking that tonight they should have just stuck to their routine.

Poppy appeared then, walking behind his children.

"They couldn't wait," she called out. "Their stomachs were rumbling like they'd never been fed!"

He grinned, then tried to stop himself. What was it about this woman? She had him smiling away as if he was the happiest guy in the world, her grin so infectious he couldn't seem *not* to return it.

"Dad, is it ready yet?" Alex was looking up at him as if he were beyond starving.

"We have a few technical issues, but so long as you're okay with no plates and wiping your fingers on the grass—" he nodded toward the overgrown lawn "—then we'll be fine."

Poppy came closer and took out the loaf of bread, passing a piece to each child. "Sounds fine to me," she said. "Sauce first or on the sausage?"

"Both," Katie replied.

"Well, okay then. Sauce overload it is."

Harrison tried not to look at her, but it was impossible. Even his children were acting as if they'd known her their entire lives.

He knew he should be happy. A teacher who could make his children light up like that should be commended. But there was something about her that worried him.

Because there was no going back from this. If she left, then…it wasn't even worth thinking about.

All he could do was get to know her and make sure he did everything within his power to convince her to stay.

He cleared his throat and passed her the first sausage, which she covered with lashings of ketchup.

If only he could stop staring at the way her mouth had a permanent uptilt, the way her eyes lit up every time she spoke or listened to his children or the way her ponytail fell over her shoulder and brushed so close to her breasts that he was struggling to avert his eyes. Because none of those things were going to help him.

Just because he hadn't been around a beautiful woman for longer than he could remember didn't give him any excuse to look at her that way. Besides, he was sworn off women...for life.

"So what do I need to know about Bellaroo?"

Harrison blinked and looked at Poppy, her head tipped slightly to the side as she looked up at him.

"What do you want to know?"

Poppy wrapped Alex's sausage in bread before doing her own and joining them on the grass. It was parched and yellowed and in definite need of some TLC, but she didn't mind sitting on it. Besides, it was either that or the concrete, so she didn't really have a choice.

"So what's happened to this place? I mean, is it just that too many families moved away from here, or is there something else going on that I don't know about?" she asked Harrison.

He was chewing, and she watched the way his Adam's apple bobbed up and down, the strong, chiseled angle of his jaw as he swallowed.

She needed to stop staring. For a girl who'd moved here to get away from men, she sure wasn't behaving like it.

"Are you asking me if the town is haunted? Or if some gruesome crime happened here and made all the residents flee?"

Harrison's tone was serious, but there was a playful glint to his eyes that made her glare at him mockingly.

"Well, I can tell you right now that I searched the place online for hours but couldn't come up with anything juicy," she teased in return. "So if it's been hidden that well, I guess I can't expect you to spill your guts straight off the bat."

Now it was Harrison laughing, and she couldn't help but smile back at him. His face changed when he was happy—became less brooding and more open. He was handsome, she couldn't deny, but when he grinned he was…pretty darn gorgeous. Even if she did hate to admit that about a man right now.

"Honest truth?"

Poppy nodded, following his gaze and watching his children as they whispered to each other, leaning over and looking at something in the long grass.

Harrison drew his knees up higher and fixed his gaze in the distance. "It's hard to bring fresh blood into rural towns these days, and most of the young people that leave here don't come back. Same with all small towns." He glanced at her, plucking at a blade of grass. "I've stayed because I don't want to walk away from the land that's been in my family for generations. It means something to know the history of a place, to walk the same path as your father and your grandfather before him. This town means a lot to me, and it means a lot to every other family living here, too."

Poppy nodded. "Everyone I've met so far seems so passionate about Bellaroo," she told him earnestly. "And I really do believe that if you fight hard enough, then this town will still be here by the time *you're* a grandfather."

He shrugged. "I wish I was as positive as you are, but honestly?" Harrison sighed. "I never should have spoken to you the way I did earlier, because if you don't stick around, then there's no chance we'll be able to keep our school open. And that'll mean the end of our town, period." He blew out a big breath. "Being sole-charge teacher to a bunch of five- to eleven-year-olds isn't for the fainthearted, but if you do stay? There won't be a person in Bellaroo who won't love you."

Now it was Poppy sighing. Because she didn't need all this pressure, the feeling that everything was weighing on her shoulders.

Before she'd moved here, she'd taken responsibility for everything, had tried to fix things that were beyond being repaired. And now here she was all over again, in a make-or-break situation, when all she wanted to do was settle in to a gentler pace of life and try to figure out what her own future held.

"Sorry, I've probably said way too much."

Poppy smiled at Harrison's apology. "It's okay. I appreciate you being honest with me."

The kids ran over and interrupted. "Can we go back and finish the room?"

"Of course." Poppy stood up and offered Harrison a hand, clasping his palm within her fingers. She hardly had to take any of his weight, because he was more than capable of pushing up to his feet without assistance. But the touch of his skin against hers, the brightness of his gaze when he locked eyes with her, made her feel weak, started shivers shaking down her spine.

"How about I join you in the classroom after I've tidied up here?"

Poppy retrieved her hand and looked away, not liking how he was watching her or how she was feeling. "Sure thing. Come on, kids."

She placed a hand on Alex's shoulder and walked with them the short distance to her new classroom.

Their dad was gruff and charming at the same time, and it wasn't something she wanted to be thinking about. Not at all.

She was here to teach and to find herself. To forget her past as best she could and create a new life for herself. *Alone.*

Which meant not thinking about the handsome rancher about to join her in her classroom.

"Wow."

Poppy looked down, paper stars between her teeth as she stood on a chair and stuck the last of them to the wall. There was already a row strung from the ceiling, but she was determined to cover some old stains on the wall to complete the effect she was trying to create.

"Your children are like little worker bees," she mumbled, trying to talk without losing one of the stars.

"Little worker bees who've started to fade," he replied.

Poppy glanced back in his direction and saw that he'd scooped Alex up into his arms. The young boy wasn't even pretending he was too big to be cuddled, and had his head happily pressed to his father's chest as he watched her.

"It's getting pretty late. Why don't you head home? I'll be fine here." She wobbled on the chair, but righted herself before it tipped.

"How about we give you a lift home?"

Poppy shook her head. "It's only a short walk. I'll be fine, honestly."

Harrison didn't look convinced. "What else do you need to do here?"

Hmm. "I want the kids to walk in tomorrow and not be able to stop smiling," she told him. "So I need to put the glue glitter over the hearts in the middle, and the same with the border over there—" she pointed "—because that's where I'm going to write all their names in the morning when they arrive, in their favorite colors."

She heard Harrison sigh. Which made it even crazier when, from the corner of her eye, she saw him put his son down on his feet and pick up a gold glitter pen.

"Is this what you use for the fancy border thing?" he asked.

Poppy took the remaining paper stars from between her teeth and bit down on her lower lip to stop herself from smiling. She nodded, watching as Harrison walked to the wall and started to help.

"Like this? Kind of big, so it's obvious?"

"Yep, just like that," she said, still trying to suppress laughter.

From what she'd seen of him so far, she had a feeling he'd just storm out and leave her if she made fun of him for using the glitter, and she didn't mind the help. Not at all. Even if a masculine rancher wouldn't have been her first choice in the artistic department.

She stepped down and pushed her chair back behind

her desk before finding the silver glitter and covering some shapes at the other end of the wall from Harrison.

"Daddy, we didn't eat the cake," called out a sleepy-sounding Katie.

Poppy had forgotten all about the cake. She moved back to look at the wall, pleased with the progress they'd made. The children could help her decorate it more in the morning, but for now it looked good.

"How about we finish up and reward ourselves with a piece? What do you say?" she asked.

Harrison passed her the pen as his kids nodded. "Only problem is we don't have a knife."

She gave him a wink. "But I have a pocketknife. That'll do, right?"

He stared at her, long and hard. "Yeah, that'll do."

Poppy pulled it out and passed it to him, careful not to let their skin connect this time. "Well, let's each have a big piece, huh? I think we all deserve it."

And hopefully, it would distract her, too. Because she might be done with men, but she sure wasn't done with chocolate.

CHAPTER THREE

"THANKS FOR THE ride." Poppy swung her door shut and waved to the children in the back. She didn't expect to hear another one open and close.

"I'll walk you to the door."

What? She hadn't ever had a man walk her to the door just to be chivalrous.

"Thanks, but I'm fine. It's not like we're in the city and I'm at risk of being mugged," she joked.

The look on his face was anything but joking. "I'm not going to drive you home and not walk you to the door. It wasn't how I was raised, and if I want my daughter to grow up expecting manners, and my son to have them, then I want to make sure I set a damn good example."

"Well, when you put it like that…" She smiled at Harrison, shaking her head as she did so.

"I know I'm old-fashioned, but then so is this place. You'll realize that pretty soon, Ms. Carter."

"There's nothing wrong with old-fashioned," she said. And there wasn't; she just wasn't used to it. "Except, of course, when it comes to plumbing."

His eyebrows pulled together as he frowned. "You having problems with this place?"

She waved her hand toward the door as they reached it. "The shower produces just a pathetic drizzle of water, and the hot doesn't last for long. But for the price I'm paying I wasn't exactly expecting a palace."

"I'll see what I can do," he told her.

"Honestly, I shouldn't have said anything. Everything's fine."

Harrison stood a few steps away, cowboy hat firmly planted on his head, feet spread apart and a stern look on his face. "I'll take a look myself, check it out. Maybe later in the week."

"If you're certain?" She didn't want him going out of his way, but if he could work his magic on the shower she'd be more than grateful.

"I'm certain," he replied. "You take good care of my kids at school and I'll make sure your house doesn't fall down around you. Deal?"

"Deal." This guy was really something. "You better get those children home. Thanks for all your help tonight. I'm glad you came back."

"So we could start off on the right foot second time around?" he asked, one side of his mouth tilting into a smile.

"Yeah, something like that. And thanks for the lift."

Harrison tipped his hat and walked backward, waiting until she'd gone inside before he turned away. Poppy leaned on the doorjamb and watched him get into the car and drive slowly off, trying hard not to think about how nice he was.

Considering she'd wanted to make a voodoo doll of him and stab it after his comments earlier in the afternoon, she'd actually enjoyed his company. Or maybe it was just that his children were really sweet.

She shut and locked the door.

Who was she kidding? The guy was handsome and charming, or at least he had been this evening, and she was terrified of how quickly she'd gone from hating the entire male population to thinking how sexy the rancher dad was.

And she couldn't help but wonder why the children had never mentioned their mom and why he'd never spoken about the wife that was surely waiting at home for them.

Poppy walked down the hall and opened the fridge, reaching in for the milk and pouring some into a pot to heat. There was no microwave, so it was old-fashioned hot chocolate.

A scratching made her stop. Another noise made a shiver lick her spine.

Poppy reached for another pot and crept slowly toward the back door. She was sure she'd locked it, but... She jumped. Another scratching sound.

She slowly pulled the blind back and looked outside, flicking the light on with her other hand. If someone was out there, who was she going to call for help?

Meow.

It was a cat. Poppy put the pot down and unlocked the door, standing back and peering out into the pool of light in the backyard.

"Are you hungry?" she asked, knowing it was stupid to ask the cat a question but not caring.

She left the door open and walked back for the milk, taking a saucer and tipping some in. Poppy placed the dish inside the back door and waited. It didn't take long for the black cat to sniff the air and decide it was worth coming in, placing one white paw on the timber floor, looking around and then walking to the saucer.

Poppy shut the door and relocked it. The cat was skinny, and she wasn't going to turn him out if he had nowhere to go.

"Want to sleep on my bed?"

The cat looked up at her as he lapped the milk and she went back to stirring her own, adding some chocolate to melt in the pot with it.

"I think we'll get on just fine, you and I," she said. "Unless you go shack up with someone better looking or younger than me down the road. Then I'll know my life's *actually* over. Okay?"

The cat stayed silent.

Black cats were supposed to be bad luck. Heaven help her if there was any more of *that* coming her way. Because she'd had enough bad luck lately to last her a lifetime and then some.

"Come on, kitty," she said, pouring her hot chocolate into a large mug. "Let's go to bed."

Harrison pulled onto the dirt road that led to Black Station and glanced in the rearview mirror. Katie and Alex were both asleep in the back, oblivious to everything going on around them, and he didn't mind one bit. All he wanted was for them to be happy, because if they were happy, *he* was happy.

And they had had a pretty nice evening.

He pushed all thoughts of their new teacher from his mind, but struggled to keep her out of it. She'd been kind, sweet, polite—not to mention the fact that she was the prettiest woman he'd seen in years—but there was still something about her niggling away at him. Something that meant he didn't believe she'd be able to stay. Or maybe it was just that he didn't believe anyone could stick it out here unless they'd been born and bred in a rural town.

His wife sure hadn't. And part of him believed that if a mother couldn't even stay to care for her own children, then Poppy Carter wouldn't stay for other people's children. Maybe he'd expected someone older, someone less attractive. Not a woman in her late twenties with long, straight hair falling down her back and bright blue eyes that seemed to smile every time she looked at his children. Not a beautiful, modern woman who looked as if she should be lunching with friends or shopping in her spare time.

But then, maybe he was being unfair. Just because she liked to look pretty and wear nice clothes didn't mean she wouldn't be able to make a life here for herself. For all he knew she could have her own personal demons that had sent her scurrying away from her former life.

Harrison pulled up outside the house and went to open the door before going back to the truck to carry his children one at a time into their bedrooms. They might be five and seven years old now, but they were still his babies. He'd raised them himself and he was determined to fight to keep their school open. Because he wouldn't ever let them feel as if they'd been abandoned, and that meant boarding school wasn't an option he was willing to consider, not until they were ready for high school.

Their mom had walked out on them, and he didn't ever want them to think he'd do the same. They were his children, his flesh and blood, and he would do anything in his power to protect them. No matter what.

But if he could fix up the teacher's house and make life a little easier for her here in Bellaroo Creek, then he would do it. Because instead of pushing her away, he was going to do everything within his power to convince her to stay.

He'd like to think that his reasons were based purely on keeping his children happy. He had a feeling that part of him, some deep, dark part that was hidden away under lock and key, liked the look of Poppy. A lot. Even if he wouldn't ever be ready to admit it.

Old Mrs. Jones had been right. Poppy arriving in their town was like a beaming ray of sunshine descending upon the place, and they were long overdue for someone like her to be their lucky charm. It wasn't just his children at stake here, it was the future of their entire town.

Poppy Carter was going to keep Bellaroo Creek alive, or she was going to be the final straw that closed the area for good. He just had to believe that she was going to be their falling star—the once-in-a-lifetime teacher that they had only ever dreamed of.

Harrison shook his head and flicked the television on, falling onto the sofa. Maybe he'd been reading too many fairy tales to Katie. Because he was actually starting to believe that maybe Poppy was that person, after all.

Poppy's stomach had a permanent flutter in it. She'd barely been able to eat any breakfast, she was so nervous, and now she was sitting in her chair, thrumming her fingers across the timber surface of her desk.

She sat and stared at the wall they'd decorated the night before, smiling as she thought of big, gruff Harrison using her fairy glitter so they could finish up and head home. She'd met lots of great dads in her time as a teacher, but even she hadn't expected him to volunteer with *glitter*.

The slam of a car door made her snap to attention. *It was happening.* Her first day as sole teacher of Bellaroo Creek School had officially begun.

Poppy stood and crossed the room, pinning the door back to welcome the first of her pupils. A smiling mom was headed her way, three children running ahead of her, straight toward Poppy.

"Slow down!"

She grinned as their mom yelled at them. They skidded to a halt in front of her just before they reached the door.

"Hi, kids. I'm Ms. Carter, your new teacher."

The three boys looked up at her, not saying a word,

but she could tell straight away from their cheeky expressions that they were going to be a handful.

"Hi."

Poppy held out her hand. "You must be pleased school's starting," she said, touching the mother's shoulder before stepping back. "I know how exhausting three boys can be."

"I just hope they don't send you running for the hills. Twenty kids each day would drive me crazy."

Poppy shook her head. "I do this because I love it, so don't worry about a few rowdy children scaring me away." She looked across the yard and saw a familiar truck pulling in close to the curb. "Besides, I'm told the lovely Mrs. Leigh volunteers one day a week as teacher aide." Poppy waved a hand. "Here are the Black children, nice and early."

The other woman followed her gaze. "You've met the Black family already?"

Poppy couldn't look away if she tried. She could see Harrison turn in the driver's seat, talking to his children, before he pushed open his door and went around to help them out.

"I haven't met Mrs. Black yet, but the children seem lovely." She couldn't drag her gaze from Harrison as he strode toward them, schoolbags slung over his shoulder, eyes locked on hers. Katie skipped along ahead of him, little Alex at his side.

"Honey, there is no Mrs. Black," the other woman teased. "Harrison is dad of the year in Bellaroo. His wife left him with the kids when Alex was a baby, so he's kind of a legend around here. We call him Mr. Sexy and Single."

Poppy gulped. He was single?

She looked away and concentrated her energies on the mom she was talking to. "I never caught your name?"

"Pat. And my boys are Scott, John and Sam." She smiled and took a few steps backward. "It was great meeting you. I'll see you this afternoon at pickup."

Poppy waved goodbye and turned to face the next parent...who just happened to be Harrison. Katie gave her a wave and ran straight through the door, but Alex stayed close to his dad.

"Morning," Poppy said brightly. "How are you, Alex?"

He looked a little shy, but managed a smile.

"He had only one term in school last year, so it's all a bit daunting."

Poppy knelt down, pleased to be closer to his son than the man towering over them. "Sweetheart," she said, tucking her fingers gently under his chin to tilt it up. "I'll look after you all day, so you don't need to worry. You can even come and sit with me if you're scared, okay?"

He nodded.

"Why don't you run in and play with the other kids?" Poppy asked him.

Alex threw his arms around his dad's leg before doing as she'd suggested.

"Thanks," Harrison said, his voice gruff.

"No problem. It's what I do."

They stood awkwardly, and she couldn't stop thinking about the fact that he'd raised both his children on his own. It wasn't often she heard of a dad being in that position. No wonder he'd been in no rush to get home last night—it wasn't as if he'd had a wife waiting for him.

Another vehicle pulled up and a few kids climbed out.

"I'd better get in there," Poppy said, nodding toward the classroom.

Harrison touched a few fingers to the rim of his hat.

"And thanks again for last night. I really appreciated your help," she added.

He walked a couple of steps away before turning around and looking straight into her eyes. "I'll fix up that plumbing for you after school when I come to collect the kids."

Poppy swallowed. Hard. Maybe it was because she knew he was available, that he wasn't some other woman's husband.

Because if he were, she'd *never* let herself think about him the way she was right now…not ever. She knew how it felt to be the other woman, so even thinking about married men inappropriately was forbidden as far as she was concerned.

But now… Harrison was as handsome as any man she'd ever laid eyes upon, and the way his jeans clung to his butt when he walked away, the cowboy hat on his head, his checked shirtsleeves rolled up to show off tanned arms…it was making her think all kinds of sin.

"You must be Ms. Carter!"

Poppy blinked and tried to forget all about the man walking toward his truck. She was a teacher, and she had more parents to meet.

She'd be seeing Harrison again after school, and he'd be in her home. In her bathroom.

So no more thinking about him until then.

CHAPTER FOUR

Poppy sat with Katie and Alex, watching out for their dad to arrive. He was only a few minutes late. The other children had all gone right on time, and now she was enjoying the sun and the company.

"Here he comes!" Alex called out, and ran to the edge of the pavement, waving to his dad.

Harrison jumped out and scooped his son straight up and into his arms. "I'm so sorry, Poppy," he said, running a hand through his hair as if he'd just realized he didn't have his hat on. "I had a run-in with a pretty pissed-off bull, and—"

"Daddy!" Katie had her hands on her hips. "You said a bad word," she hissed, "and she's our teacher, so you need to call her Ms. Carter."

He nodded as if she was absolutely right, but when his eyes met Poppy's they were filled with laughter. She had to bite down on her lip to stop from laughing herself.

"Anyway, long story short, he was determined to make his way to the ladies, which wasn't going to happen," Harrison told her.

Poppy did burst out laughing then—she couldn't help it. She was talking to a real-life cowboy when she'd never even been close to a real ranch before. "Do you have any idea how hilarious that sounds?"

He gave her a puzzled look. "Funny now, but not so amusing when you're staring a three-thousand-pound, adrenaline-filled beast in the eye."

She started to walk alongside Katie as they all headed for the truck. "Harrison, the closest I've come to dealing with wildlife is an ant infestation in my old classroom," she told him. "So believe me when I tell you how hilarious you sound to my sheltered city ways. Hilarious, but exciting, for a change."

She could have sworn a dark look passed across his face, but it was gone so quickly she couldn't be certain. Had she said something wrong?

"Although in saying that, I did kind of adopt a cat last night, so maybe I'm getting used to the whole country way of life already."

Harrison opened the front passenger door to his truck, but pointed for Katie to get in the back. "What do you mean, you adopted a cat? It's not like we have shelters for unwanted pets around here."

Poppy rolled her eyes, wishing she wasn't standing quite so close to him. He was at least a head taller than her, and she couldn't stop staring back into his dark brown eyes. They were dark but soft, like melted chocolate.

She snapped herself out of her daydream. Could she really forgive the entire male population so soon after declaring them all to be worthless idiots to whom she'd never again give the time of day? The answer to that question was no.

"I heard a noise last night and a black cat was just sitting there, like it was his house and he wanted to come in."

"But not wild?" Harrison asked. He gestured for her to get in the vehicle. "I'll drive you down the road— you know, so I can fix the bathroom."

Heat hit Poppy's cheeks and she hoped the blush wasn't noticeable. What was it about this guy getting her all in a fluster, especially at the mention of coming into her home? And the thought of sitting beside him in such a close space, despite the fact that his children were in the back.

"I don't think a wild cat would have slept the night on my bed," she told him, glancing down at his hand as he took command of the gear stick. His skin was a deep brown from what she imagined was hours out in the sun each day, and his forearm looked muscular. She tried to switch her focus to the road ahead. "Actually, I take that back. He slept on my pillow."

The children were chatting away in the rear, but she was listening only to their father. The man she couldn't seem to tear her eyes away from no matter how hard she tried.

"You're a real sucker, you know that?" Harrison's eyes crinkled in the corners, gentle wrinkles forming as he laughed at her. "Definitely not a country girl yet."

"I'd like to think I'm kindhearted," she replied.

He shrugged. "Same thing, if you ask me. But it's

weird that a cat just appeared out of nowhere. He must belong to someone."

"I told him he was welcome to stay, but I left a window open so he could come and go."

"And you're not pretending he's yours?" Harrison asked, one hand on the wheel, the other slung out the window.

"Exactly."

"You named him yet?"

"Lucky," she said. "Because I don't believe that black cats are bad luck, and he was lucky to find me and my large pitcher of milk."

"He's yours," Harrison said with a laugh. "Once you name them you're committed. Happens every time."

Poppy laughed with him, because he was right, and because it felt nice not to feel sad for once. She'd spent the past month wondering what the hell she was going to do with her life, how she was going to rebuild everything she'd lost, and that hadn't left much time for just laughing and being happy.

But Bellaroo Creek was her fresh start. It was her place to start over. So if she felt like laughing, then she wasn't going to hold back.

Harrison was lying on his back, squished half inside a cupboard, with his wrench jammed on the fitting he was trying to tighten. He tried to ignore the swear words sitting on the tip of his tongue, shifting his body instead to get a better look at the leak.

"Harrison?"

Crap. He'd been in such a dream world that he

hadn't expected anyone to walk in on him, and now he'd smacked his head on the underside of the cupboard.

"Are you okay? Did you hurt yourself?"

Harrison grunted and shuffled out of the small space. He touched his head. "No blood, so I'll live."

He stared up at Poppy, who was wringing her hands together as if she wasn't quite sure what to say.

"I, um, was wondering if you'd like to stay for dinner? I mean, you've been working in here for a while and I think the kids are getting hungry...."

"I'm not gonna let this beat me. You know that, right?" Even if he still had no idea why this darn plumbing was causing her such a problem every time she switched on anything in the bathroom.

"I didn't mean that you were taking too long, because I really do appreciate it, but..."

"Sure." Harrison shrugged. She was babbling like a crazy woman, or as if she was...nervous. He doubted that, especially after the way she'd stood up to him the day before, sassing at him for speaking his mind. "After wrangling these pipes, I think dinner would be great."

She smiled. As if she'd asked him a tough question and he'd miraculously given her an answer.

"Well, that's settled then. I'll go tell the children."

Poppy turned and walked away, and Harrison sat on her bathroom floor and watched her go. There was something about her, something getting under his skin that he didn't want to acknowledge. Something that had made him offer to fix her plumbing, made him say yes to dinner, all those things.

And it was something he didn't want to figure out.

She was his children's schoolteacher, a new woman in the community, but that was all. Because he wasn't looking for anything other than friendship in his life. His kids meant everything to him, and getting involved with a woman wasn't in his future.

So why was he still sitting on the floor so he could watch her walk down the hall?

Poppy watched the children as they lay on their stomachs, legs crossed at the ankles while they stared at the television. She'd already given them crisps and orange juice, and now she was cooking dinner while they watched a cartoon and their father worked on the bathroom.

The old house was like nothing she was used to, and it was taking all her patience to work in the tiny kitchen, but in a way it was nice. Nice to be cooking for more than just one, to have had a great first day at school and to feel as if her life was finally moving in the right direction again.

"Something smells good."

The deep, sexy voice coming from behind her made her hand freeze in midmotion. Hearing him speak put her almost as much on edge as looking at him did, no matter how much she wanted to pretend that she was just the teacher and he was just the father of two of her pupils.

"It's nothing fancy, just pasta," she told him, resuming her stirring.

She listened as Harrison walked into the kitchen, felt his presence in the too-small space.

"It smells fancy."

Poppy watched as he came closer and stood beside her. He peered into the pan, using the wooden spoon she'd discarded to give the contents a gentle stir.

"Garlic and bacon," she said, moving away slightly, needing to put some distance between them. Anything at all to stop her heart from racing a million miles an hour and quell the unease in her stomach. "I fry it in some oil before adding the sauce and tossing in the pasta."

He nodded and put the spoon back where he'd found it, leaning against a cupboard and watching her cook.

"Anything not working in here?" he asked.

"Ah, no. Everything seems to be fine."

"You don't sound so sure."

What she was sure about was needing him to look away, to go sit with his children instead of fixing his eyes on her while she was trying to concentrate.

"It's fine. Everything works okay, I guess. It's just different," she confessed.

"To what you're used to?"

Poppy sighed, then shrugged. "I've had a fancy kitchen and a modern apartment, and it didn't make me happy, so I'm not going to let a rustic kitchen get me down." It was the truth, and now she'd said it. "Lighting the gas with a match before I cook isn't going to bother me so long as I can do a job I love and wake up with a smile on my face each day."

Harrison was still staring at her, but his expression had lost the intensity of before. There was a softness in his eyes now, almost as if he understood what she was trying to say. What she was trying to get across to him.

"There's something to be said for smiling in the mornings," he told her.

Poppy looked away, not because she was embarrassed, but because she didn't know what to say. When she'd chosen to come here, she'd decided to keep her past exactly that—she didn't want it to define her future and didn't want everyone knowing her business. But it sure was hard to get to know someone without thinking about what her life had been like only a month earlier.

"What's for dinner?" Katie appeared in the kitchen, rising on tiptoe as she tried to see what was cooking.

"Pasta with a carbonara sauce," Poppy told her, using her elbow to playfully push her from the kitchen. "Hang out with Alex for a few more minutes and it'll be ready."

The little girl grinned, gave her dad a cheeky wave and disappeared again.

"You might think this is nothing fancy," said Harrison, pointing at the sauce Poppy was stirring, "but to them it's fun to be somewhere different for dinner. They're usually just stuck with me on the ranch."

She swallowed a lump. It was now or never, and she couldn't help herself.

"So there's no Mrs. Black?" she asked, knowing full well what the answer was going to be.

"No," Harrison replied, his eyes dark and stormy, his expression like stone. "There's no Mrs. Black, unless you're talking about my mom."

If only her question was that innocent, but they both

knew it wasn't. What Poppy didn't know was why she'd asked at all.

Maybe she just wanted to hear it from him, so she could actually believe that he didn't have a wife…that he really was what the mom today had described him as—the town's sexiest bachelor.

Sauce. What Poppy needed to do was focus on the carbonara sauce.

"Anything I can do?" His soft, deep drawl made her skin go hot, then suddenly cold, as if an icy breeze had blown through on a warm summer's day.

"I'd love for you to put those plates on the table," she said, nodding toward where she had them stacked. "And to be honest, I wouldn't mind celebrating my first day at school with a glass of wine."

Plus she wouldn't mind settling her nerves a little with the bottle of sauvignon blanc she had in the fridge.

"Glasses?" he asked, carrying the plates to the table.

Poppy groaned. "Still to be unpacked, I think." One of the few things she hadn't actually transferred from box to cupboard. But if she wasn't mistaken… "Hang on, try the box at the bottom of the pantry," she instructed. "I can't leave this sauce."

Harrison strode across the kitchen in a few long steps, commanding her attention. As if she needed more distracting.…

"This box?"

She nodded. "Yep, that's the one."

She dragged her eyes from him and focused on the food again. She took the sauce from the stove, added the cooked pasta to the pot she had waiting and poured all the sauce in, too. She gently tossed it, refusing to give the dinner she'd cooked any less attention than it deserved. This was one of her favorite comfort foods, although she usually did the pasta from scratch when she personally needed comforting, and she was just hoping the Black family would like what she'd rustled up.

Harrison poured wine into the two glasses he'd found and placed them on the table before going to herd his kids in for dinner. They were still mesmerized by the television.

"Let's go, dinner's ready."

Katie had the adopted black cat on her lap, stroking it over and over again, and it was purring so loudly he could hear it from the doorway.

"Put the fleabag down and come sit up," he ordered, trying not to smile at the horrified look his daughter was giving him. "On second thought, perhaps you should wash your hands first."

"It's okay, Lucky," Katie crooned to the cat. "Don't listen to *anything* he says, all right?"

He watched as she placed the cat down gently, as if he was breakable, before standing up and flouncing past him. More teenager than kid.

"He is *not* a *fleabag*," she hissed.

"I was just teasing, sweetheart. Now go wash up, then sit at the table for dinner." Harrison gestured for his son to do the same, then joined Poppy back in the kitchen.

"Finally ready," she told him, her cheeks flushed from standing over the range.

He jumped forward to take the large dish from her, their hands colliding as his fingers closed around it. "Let me take this."

Poppy's eyes met his, blue irises flashing to the food and back to him again, as if she had no idea what to say or why they were standing so close.

"Thanks," she finally said, taking a step back while brushing the hair from her face and tucking it behind her ears.

Harrison transported the dish to the table, wishing he didn't feel quite so comfortable being in this woman's house. He was used to telling himself why he didn't need female company in his life, why he was better off alone, but Poppy was reminding him of all the reasons his thinking could be flawed.

What his wife had done to him, the way she'd hurt him, would never go away. But it didn't mean he needed to feel guilty for spending an evening in the company of the new local teacher. So long as he protected his children from being hurt again, he had nothing to fear.

"Katie seems very fond of animals," Poppy said, making him turn.

She walked to the edge of the table and reached for her glass of wine, taking a small sip.

Harrison pulled out his chair but waited for her to sit down first. His children came bounding back into the room and jumped into their seats before he had a chance to do the same for them.

"Katie loves animals more than anyone I've ever met," he told Poppy, grinning at his daughter across the table. "I tease her about it, but she has a real way with them. Has had since she was little."

Poppy reached for Alex's plate and started to dish out their meals. "Do you like helping your dad on the ranch, Katie?"

She nodded. "Yeah, but I don't like it when it's calving time and some of the babies don't have a mom, 'cause then they're just like me, except they don't have a dad, either."

Harrison's body went tense. No matter how hard he tried, he couldn't help the jolt of anger that hit him just hearing his little girl say those words. "It's one of the reasons we have quite a few pet calves," he said, pushing the fury away and taking a deep breath. "Because Katie is so good at caring for them."

"So you help nurse them?" Poppy asked his daughter.

If she'd noticed the bitterness flashing through him, she did a good job of disguising it. Just when he thought he was over his anger at their mother for leaving the kids, Katie went and said something like that.

"Daddy lets me feed them with a bottle, and we get to name them," Katie said, smiling as Poppy passed her a plate full of pasta.

"Which is why we have an entire field full of pet cows," Harrison explained, smiling across at his daughter. "As I tell the kids, as soon as you name them it's very hard to say goodbye."

"Because they get made into steak," Katie announced.

Poppy's eyes met his. He was certain she hadn't been expecting *that* response.

"That's right." Harrison twirled his fork into his pasta and tasted it. "And this," he said, pausing to swallow his mouthful, "tastes as great as it smells."

Poppy's eyes were still trained on him. "So that's why you told me off for naming the cat."

"Exactly."

She grinned and held up her glass. "I meant to say a toast before we started."

Harrison touched his napkin to his lips and followed her lead. "Sure."

Poppy raised her glass. "To surviving my first day of school and to new friends."

He nodded. "And to me winning the fight with the bull today." Harrison winked at her across the table, then wished he could take it back. Why the hell had he done that?

Because it had come naturally, and he hadn't even thought about it. Even though he hadn't flirted with anyone for longer than he could remember.

Poppy was staring straight down at her plate now, focused on her food, and he felt like a fool for embarrassing her. Especially after she'd been so nice, asking them to stay for a meal.

"So what do you think of Bellaroo so far?" he asked, trying to keep the topic neutral. "Everything you thought it would be?"

Poppy laughed, holding her hand in front of her mouth. He kept eating and waited for her to reply, tuning out the chatter from Katie and Alex. From what he could gather they were arguing about the name for the next orphaned calf.

"I guess I didn't realize how quiet it would be here," Poppy told him frankly.

"You never did visit before you took the job, did you?" he asked, knowing the answer but wanting to hear it from her.

"I just trusted my gut that it was the right place for me," she said. "And I was told there were no other applicants, so I didn't exactly have to audition for the part."

Harrison could tell from the shine in her eyes that she was upset—that just talking about her move here had touched a nerve—yet she'd tried to joke her way out of it.

"At the time, I thought it was a sign, because I needed to get away from…" Her voice trailed off, as if she was trying to decide whether or not to tell him the truth.

"I didn't mean to pry," Harrison said, knowing what it was like to want to keep a secret, to want to keep memories buried.

"You're not," she said, touching a knuckle to each eye, pushing away the first hint of a tear. "They're questions that I'm going to be asked, and I want to answer them honestly."

Was she a criminal? Had something happened in her past that they should have known about before they gave her the job at the school?

Harrison picked up his fork again and continued to eat, more for something to do than the fact that he was still hungry. Because listening to Poppy had taken his mind off his stomach.

"Last year was a little rough for me," she admitted, playing with the edge of her napkin, yet bravely looking at him as she spoke. "I, well, my husband got us into a lot of trouble, and I lost everything I'd worked so hard for."

She was married? "You're married?" How had she not mentioned this earlier, and why the hell did he care, anyway?

Poppy grimaced. "Unfortunately, yes."

Wow. He hadn't even seen that coming. "So your husband won't be joining you here?"

Poppy laughed, but it didn't sound like a happy noise. "Let's just say that me coming here was as much to get away from him as anything." She shook her head and glanced at the children. "One day I'll tell you all about it."

Maybe they had more in common than he'd realized. "We could trade crappy spouse and divorce stories," he joked. Unless she'd walked out on her man, as his wife had him....

"Believe me, mine's up there with the best of them."

Harrison grinned, relieved. "Yep, me, too."

Poppy stood at her front door and waved as Harrison pulled away from the curb and headed for home. It had been a nice evening, and she was pleased she'd asked them to stay, but she was still thinking about their conversation over dinner.

She'd told herself over and over again that talking about her husband wasn't productive, that she'd be better off pretending he didn't exist. But doing so was easier than *saying so.*

After the way Chris had hurt her, the lies, the pain...

Poppy shuddered and shut the door behind her, leaning against it and sliding all the way to the floor.

The man she'd pledged to spend the rest of her life with, the one person in the world she'd trusted above all else, had hurt her so badly that it still took her breath away.

Tears fell slowly down her cheeks, drizzling down her jaw. Poppy shut her eyes, tried to force the memories away, but nothing worked. The cold shiver that took over her body whenever she thought about him descended, as it always did.

And she was alone. After thinking she'd found her soul mate, trusting him like she'd never trusted anyone before, she was alone. And she was broke.

She'd lost her apartment, her husband and everything else she'd worked so hard for. But she wasn't going to let it define who she was, because the one thing he hadn't taken from her was her future. And the person she was, beneath everything she'd lost.

"I'm healthy. I'm a teacher. I make a difference," Poppy whispered, eyes still shut tight as she repeated the words that always got her through her pain.

A meow made her blink away her tears. The cat was sitting near her feet, staring at her as if he was trying to figure out what the heck she was doing on the floor in the hall.

"And I'm a mom," she whispered, pulling herself to her feet and bending to pick up the cat.

Even if it wasn't to the baby she'd been so excited about carrying.

"A cat's better than no one," she told her new furry friend.

And she could tell him everything without fearing the consequences.

CHAPTER FIVE

HARRISON CURSED AT his dog as she ran out and disobeyed his command. He went to yell at her, then stopped himself. Just because he was in a crappy mood didn't mean his dog deserved to be scolded. He could see from the look on her face that she was confused.

"Go way back," he instructed, giving up on his whistling.

The dog glanced at him before following his command, perfectly this time. He walked up slowly, waited for her to push the last few cattle through then closed the gate behind them.

"Good girl," he said, giving her a pat on the head when she settled against his leg, bright eyes connecting with his. "You did good."

Harrison sat down on the grass and stretched his legs out in front of him. The dog lay at his side. He worked Suzy on her own only when they were dealing with a small herd or the odd rogue cattle beast, and she stuffed up only when he stuffed up. And he knew why he was showing himself up today—because there was a certain teacher on his mind he couldn't forget about, and because his daughter was going to be furious with him when she got home.

He was never, ever again going to let her help him with the young stock. What had started as something nice to do together, spending time with his girl and teaching her the ropes, helping her to deal with the confusion of not having her own mom, had turned into him letting her save a heap of calves that he was lumped with for the foreseeable future.

So much for being a tough rancher. One burst of tears from Katie and he'd promised the orphans wouldn't be sent away, even though he knew he couldn't keep them forever.

But he'd solved the biggest part of the problem— separating the bull calf from the females before he became an issue. And lucky for Katie, he was good enough to be considered for stud. Although a half-tame bull might be scarier than a wild one when it came to mating time.

Mating. Why the hell had Harrison thought about that when he was struggling not to wonder why the hell Poppy was living in the middle of nowhere without her husband? Had she left the man? Had he done something to make her want to run? Harrison would be damned if he'd stand by and let the woman be terrified of some lowlife tracking her down.

He let out a big breath and dropped his palm to his dog's head, kneading her fur gently with his fingers. She was his best form of stress relief because he relied on her and she never answered back, and because she was the only female he'd had affection from since his wife had left.

"Come on, girl. It's time for lunch." Then it was school pickup, and he was going to get in and out as quickly as he could. Poppy was a great teacher; his kids liked her, and hell, so did he. But being around her wasn't good for him, made him think all sorts of things that he'd sworn off thinking these past few years, and what he needed to do was distance himself. Before he started thinking up all kinds of stupid ideas and did something crazy like ask her over for dinner.

Maybe he needed to take his helicopter up for a spin, check out the far fields—anything to get his head back in the space he needed it to be in.

Poppy sat at her desk and pretended not to notice some of the girls whispering and passing notes. She wasn't about to ruin their fun, not yet at least, not when they'd already completed the task she'd set them. And besides, she wasn't quite ready to stop her own daydreaming, no matter how dangerous it might be.

Harrison Black. Why couldn't she seem to forget the way his fingers had felt against hers when they'd clashed on the dish? The look in his eyes when he'd been talking about his daughter or the cool way he'd announced there was no Mrs. Black.

Less than two months ago, Poppy had been thinking about her wedding, wondering whether to wear white or ivory, flicking through bridal magazines. Now she was virtually penniless, had had her heart broken in more ways than she could imagine and was already struggling not to think about a handsome-as-hell rancher she'd met only three times.

Poppy smiled to herself. And the first meeting hadn't exactly gone down well.

"What are you laughing about?"

She looked up and saw the girls watching her. They were no longer scribbling notes but eyeing her instead.

"I'm not laughing. I'm just smiling about how nice it is to be here," she replied, cheeks flushing ever so slightly at being caught out, especially with Katie staring at her so intently. The last thing Poppy needed was the young girl knowing she was dreaming about her father.

"Is it different here than your last school?" an older girl, Marie, asked her.

"Yes," Poppy answered, standing up so she could walk around to the front of her desk and lean back on it. "The last school I taught at was in the middle of the city, and we had a big, high fence around the outside and a concrete playground. The children had to be collected inside the gates and signed for by their parents or caregiver."

It couldn't have been more different to the relaxed attitude at Bellaroo, where all the parents knew one another on a first name basis.

"Is it better here?" another child asked.

"I wouldn't have come here if I didn't think it would be better, and I can tell you right now that it's even better than I imagined it could be."

Every child in the room was staring at her now, and

she couldn't help but smile back at their beaming little faces.

"Enough talk about me. It's time for you to share your stories. Let's start with the eldest and make our way down, okay?"

Poppy sat on the edge of her desk and waved to Connor, her eldest pupil, to come forward.

She hadn't been lying to the children; it *was* better here. In fact, old house aside, it was almost perfect.

A phone rang and she looked around. She didn't even recall there *being* a phone in the classroom, and she hadn't bothered turning her mobile phone on since she'd arrived. It had sat dormant from the moment she'd left the city behind, in fact. There wasn't a signal out here, and all the ranchers used satellite phones when they needed to communicate.

"Anyone know where the phone is?" she asked.

A few of the kids pointed to her left.

"In the cupboard?" She wasn't convinced, but sure enough, there was an ancient-looking phone attached to the wall. Poppy picked up the receiver. "Hello, Bellaroo Creek School," she said hesitantly.

"Poppy, it's Harrison."

Harrison? "Is everything okay?" He sounded out of breath and her heart picked up rhythm, starting to beat fast.

"No, I've had some bad news, and I need to head for Sydney as soon as I've given the guys instructions for the cattle."

"Sydney? I don't understand."

He sounded distracted, as if he wasn't really concentrating, not sure of what to say.

"Poppy, my dad's had a heart attack and I need to get to the hospital. I'm trying to organize someone to look after the kids, but is there any chance you could stay with them a bit later today?"

"Oh, Harrison, I'm so sorry." Tears sprang into her eyes because she knew what it was like to receive a phone call like that, to have your day going along like normal and then find out that life had thrown a curve ball that had the potential to break your heart. It had been like that when her dad died, and the only consolation was that he hadn't been witness to her losing everything.

Harrison was silent on the other end, but she could hear him breathing, as if he was running around doing something. Probably packing.

"Harrison?"

"Sorry, it's just…"

"I'll take them," she said without hesitation. "Don't worry about the children, just go. If you're okay with me taking care of them, I'll do it."

He was silent again, a long pause hanging between them before he answered. "Poppy, I can't ask you to do that. You're their teacher, and you hardly even know us."

"You didn't ask me, I offered. And I know you plenty well enough." She kept her voice low, conscious of her students listening to their conversation. "You were kind enough to help me out twice now, and I already adore your children, so just go, and don't worry about them."

"Are you sure?" His voice was deep, husky and commanding. He might be upset and needing to flee, but she could feel his strength without even seeing him. "I'd never ask you to step up like that, and it wasn't why I called."

"Just tell me how to get to your place, leave a key out and do what you have to do."

"You want to stay here?" he asked, clearly surprised.

"Wouldn't that be easier? Then the children can stick to their routine and have all their things around them."

She could almost hear his brain ticking over while he was silent. "There's dogs and chooks and…"

Poppy laughed. "I'm from the city, not another planet," she said. "I have no problem with animals and I'm sure the kids can help me out, tell me where things are, that sort of thing."

Even as she was talking she was wondering what on earth she'd done, but what other option did she have? Harrison was a solo dad with few people to call on, and his children didn't need the extra worry or stress of staying with someone else when she could care for them in their own home.

"I'll swing past on my way out of town, say goodbye to the kids and give you a map for how to get to the ranch," he said after a long pause. "And I'll organize for the dogs to be taken up to the worker's house and for all the chores to be done. I have a family living in the cottage at the moment, and there's a few guys working here full-time at the moment, too, so you won't have to worry about anything."

Poppy said goodbye and took a moment to collect

herself. She glanced at her wristwatch. There was only another forty-five minutes until the end of the school day, which meant she had some time to prepare herself mentally for the children finding out that their grand-dad was unwell and their dad was leaving. She had no idea how long he'd be away for, how long she'd be expected to stay at his ranch without him, but she'd do it.

Because the truth was she missed being part of a family, hated living in a house all on her own when she was used to having people around her every day. And staying at Harrison's ranch would be like a mini-vacation in a way, her first real taste of the Australian outback up close and personal.

Her saying yes had nothing to do with the fact that Harrison had gotten under her skin. That all she'd thought about since she'd made dinner for them was how intriguing he was; how different he was from the man she'd spent the past eight years of her life with. And how easily she could take back the vow she'd made to herself about swearing off men for good.

Poppy drew a deep breath and shut the cupboard door behind her. Every single child in the room was staring at her, no doubt wondering who she'd been talking to and what was going on.

But she wasn't going to say anything to Katie and Alex until their father arrived, because he was their dad and it was his place to explain to them what was happening.

"Okay, back to reading your stories aloud. Who was first?"

Poppy sat down at her desk and fixed a smile on her

face, even though inside she was anything but calm and happy.

She was terrified. Because she'd just volunteered to help out Harrison and his gorgeous children, and the reality of that was starting to set in. She'd be staying in his home, caring for his kids, *being part of his family.*

Poppy touched her stomach with her palm, feeling how flat it was.

If she hadn't had the miscarriage, she'd be close to having her own child, her own family...and there wasn't a day that went by that she didn't think about the child she'd lost.

Poppy kept telling herself that it would happen, that she'd be a mom one day, only she wasn't so sure she'd ever be able to find a man trustworthy enough to be the dad.

Harrison dropped a kiss on his daughter's head and gave his son another big hug.

"I'll only be a few days, okay? I just need to get to Sydney, spend some time at the hospital, then I'll come straight back home."

He felt like crap for leaving them, but what choice did he have? His parents meant a lot to him and he was their only child—he couldn't let his dad die without telling him how much he loved him. It wasn't something he'd ever told him before, and the thought of never getting the chance to be honest and say how he felt? He couldn't let that happen.

"We're going to have lots of fun while your dad's away," Poppy told the kids, meeting his gaze and giving him a reassuring smile. "Late nights, yummy food and lots of television."

Harrison nodded, hoping his smile looked genuine. "I'll be back before you even know I'm gone. It's only a five-hour drive, so if you really need me I can get home pretty fast."

They looked sad, but they understood. Or at least they seemed to better understand now that he'd explained to them why they couldn't join him and what exactly a heart attack was. He knew they'd be scared, but they were in good hands; he couldn't have found anyone he'd trust more with his children if he'd tried, even though they had known Poppy only a short time.

"You're sure then?" he asked, for what was probably the tenth time since he'd arrived at the school grounds.

"Positive."

Poppy had a sunny smile on her face, and when she stepped toward him, arms held out, he didn't back away. Couldn't. Because he was so alone right now, and the pain he was feeling at the idea of his dad hooked up to machines in a hospital was so intense it was starting to consume him. Like a hand around his neck slowly choking him, draining him of all his strength, all his determination.

"Come here," she said, folding her arms around him and enveloping him in a tight hug. "Everything's going to be okay, Harrison."

He mumbled something against her head, into her silky hair, but didn't even know what he was trying to say. What he did know was how great she felt in his arms, how soothing it was to be held. By someone warm and soft and so feminine.

"Thank you," he whispered, his voice low and gravelly as he held back tears he hadn't even known had been waiting to fall.

"I've been where you are and I know how it feels. But you need to believe it's going to be okay," she told him, squeezing him tight before stepping back a fraction.

Harrison looked down into her warm aqua eyes, noting the way soft bits of short hair were wisping around her face. Despite everything—the pain and the confusion—all he could think about when he stared at Poppy was what it would be like to kiss the breath from her, tug her back in tight against him and just kiss the hell out of those plump lips.

Her smile drew him in, made him keep his hands against her back after hugging her. Harrison bent slightly, slowly moving toward her, before he stopped himself. Glancing at his children, he realized they were watching what was happening. And if he hesitated a second longer, if he didn't let go of Poppy, it would move from an innocent hug between friends to something far murkier.

The confusion evident all over Poppy's face told him he'd already hesitated too long, but the nervous smile she gave him? That told him that maybe, just maybe, she'd been thinking exactly what he'd been thinking.

"Uh-hmm." Harrison cleared his throat and put a definite few steps between them this time, needing to get as far away from her as possible. "I'd best be off.

You two be on your best behavior for Ms. Carter, you hear me?"

"Poppy," he heard her say, then turned to watch her mouth as she spoke, drawn in again by the woman he was trying so hard to resist. "I'm more than just your teacher now, so out of school you can call me Poppy."

Maybe inviting her to stay in his home, care for his children, be his *someone* in his hour of need, had been the stupidest thing he'd ever done. *Either the stupidest or the cleverest.* He wouldn't be able to decide until he'd figured out how to resist her. Because they could never, *ever* be more than just friends.

Right now that was the only thing he was certain about.

"Love you," he told his kids, looking from Katie to Alex.

They were being so brave, standing on either side of Poppy now as he walked around to the driver's side of his truck.

"Drive safely and phone us when you get there," Poppy called out.

"Funny, but I said that to my parents when they went away. It was supposed to be their relaxing trip around Australia, taking in the sights, and they only made it to Sydney to enjoy the big city."

Poppy never took her eyes from him, and he spent a moment looking back at her. He could see every bit of the compassion she was feeling for him, as if her arms were around him, comforting him, even though she was still standing on the pavement and he was on the road.

Harrison jumped behind the wheel and waved out

the window, turning the ignition. As he drove away, he alternated between staring at the road ahead and into his rearview mirror.

It had been a long time since he'd seen a woman, aside from his own mom, embracing his children. Comforting them, caring for them, doing the things he'd had to do for so long on his own.

He'd tried to pretend that his children didn't need a mom, that they were doing fine without one and that he was enough.

So why was seeing Poppy with them, so kind and nurturing, making him feel they were missing out on more than he'd ever wanted to admit?

Harrison turned up the stereo until it was blaring and focused on the road. He had a long drive ahead of him, and thinking about his ex-wife, or Poppy, for that matter, wasn't going to make the drive any easier.

CHAPTER SIX

Poppy looked around the kitchen. She was like a fish out of water—less because she was out of her depth and more because it was weird, poking around in someone else's things. Harrison had asked her into his home, told her to make herself comfortable, but it was still kind of awkward.

Plus she'd presumed there would be enough supplies without even checking.

"What do you guys feel like for dinner?" she asked, hand poised on the fridge door.

Alex didn't even look up from the television, but Katie jumped to her feet.

"There should be stuff in the fridge," the girl told her. "Dad's really good at cooking."

Interesting. Poppy had presumed he wouldn't be a good cook, just because he was a guy. That would teach her not to be sexist.

She swung the door open and had to stop her chin from hitting the floor. Her jaw literally fell open when she saw how well stocked it was. There was a heap of vegetables, fruit, bottled things—everything she could think of and more.

"So was your dad just being polite, telling me the food I made was good the other night?" She felt like an idiot now for telling him how and what she'd been cooking when he clearly knew what he was doing in the kitchen. Unless, of course, he just made them eat boiled vegetables all the time? "What does he fix you for dinner most nights?"

Katie shrugged, reaching in for the orange juice. "He cooks, like, spicy stuff," she said, standing on a little stool that was obviously there for the children, so she could get a clean glass from the cupboard. "He said that when he was at university his roommate was from Thailand, and he taught him how to cook, so he either does Thai food or something he's made up."

Poppy couldn't help smiling. So Mr. Sexy and Single wasn't just a single-dad rancher, he was also a gourmet cook. A gourmet *Thai* cook.

"So I guess boiled vegetables aren't allowed?"

"Yuk." Katie pulled a face before going back to drinking her juice. "Hey, do you want me to show you the veggie garden?"

Poppy raised her eyebrows. "Your dad has a vegetable garden?" *When did he have time for all this?*

Katie put her glass down and took Poppy by the hand, leading her across the room. "It's actually my grandma's. She comes here to look after it, and we help Dad water it, but we eat all the vegetables because she has one at her house, too." Katie pointed out the window. "But Dad says the orchard is his because he planted all the trees."

Poppy tried not to laugh but couldn't help it. It was like someone was playing a practical joke on her.

"Hey, do you want to see my room?"

Poppy let Katie take her hand again and pull her along. The kids were coping fine, treating her like a new toy, and so long as she had fun with them she knew they'd be just fine while their dad was away.

"Do you have your own bedroom?"

"Yeah," Katie said, running ahead of her. "And this is my dad's room down here."

Poppy had that uncomfortable feeling again, as if she was doing something she shouldn't be, but she shrugged it away. "Honey, where's the spare room?"

Katie spun around. "Oh, we don't have one. Well, we kind of do, but it doesn't have a bed in it, so you can sleep in Dad's."

Oh dear. Being in Harrison's house was one thing, but in his *bed*?

She cleared her throat, her cheeks burning. "Or I could just sleep in your room?"

Katie laughed and disappeared through a doorway. Poppy followed, but her heart sank as soon as she walked into the room.

"I'm not allowed to sleep on the top bunk yet, but you can if you want to."

Poppy sighed. So it was Harrison's bachelor bed or a top bunk… "It's okay, honey. Your dad's bed will be just fine."

Katie started talking again, showing her toys, danc-

ing around the room as if she were her best friend vis-
iting on a play date. But all Poppy could think about
was being in Harrison's room, sleeping between sheets
that would smell like him, that he'd been lying in that
morning.

She shook her head, trying to push him from her
mind.

Did he sleep naked?

If Katie hadn't been watching her she'd have been
tempted to slap herself to try to snap out of it.

"I think we should get back to Alex," Poppy suggested, needing to put as much distance between her
and the bedrooms as possible. Not to mention she still
had to rustle up something for dinner.

*And stop thinking about the man whose house she
was going to be living in for the next couple days.*

"Did Dad tell you about the Aboriginal family living in our cottage?" Katie asked.

Poppy's eyebrows pulled together. "He mentioned
there was a family, but not that they were native Austra-
lians." She'd never seen their culture firsthand, but was
fascinated by their traditional beliefs and way of life.

"They're really cool," Katie told her. "You should
come meet them maybe."

"Are there any children?"

"Yeah, two boys. Same age as me. But they don't
go to school."

Poppy definitely wanted to meet them. Just because
the parents chose not to send the boys to school didn't
mean she wasn't prepared to offer them assistance if
or when they needed it.

Back in the living room now, she could see Alex hadn't moved a muscle and was still parked in front of the television.

"How about you play with Alex for a while and I'll sort dinner out, okay?" she asked Katie, needing a moment just to collect her thoughts.

Her new little friend ran into the living room, leaving Poppy standing alone. Talk about information overload. A few quiet minutes to process everything was *exactly* what she needed.

Poppy was starting to realize what hard work it was being a parent. She had both children in bed with her, snuggled tight, and she was so exhausted she just wanted to shut her eyes…only Alex was still hiccuping from the bucketload of tears he'd shed on her and her pillow.

So much for being worried about sleeping in Harrison's bed. She'd hardly had time to savor the musky smell of him on the sheets before she was joined by Katie, whimpering and needing a cuddle. Then she'd heard Alex call out, as if he'd been having a nightmare, and she'd run to him as quickly as she could. The poor little boy was missing his dad like crazy and worried sick about his granddad.

"Will he die?" Alex whispered. "Will he disappear like my mom did and never come back?"

Poppy held him tighter, snuggling him so he knew how much she cared. Just because she was exhausted didn't mean she wouldn't sit up all night comforting him if he needed her to. But explaining death to him wasn't something she was comfortable with, and neither was talking to him about his mom when she didn't know the whole story.

"Honey, I don't want you to think about anyone leaving you," Poppy said in her most soothing voice. "Why don't you tell me what you'd like to do with your granddad when he's back here again instead?"

Alex whimpered and wrapped one arm around her neck, as if wanting to make sure there was no way she could leave him.

"I want to make something for him. Something cool."

"Like a poster?" she asked, keeping her voice low to make sure they didn't wake Katie.

"Yeah. Something cool to hang above the door, and a card, too."

She could hear the change in Alex's voice, knew that distracting him was probably the best thing she could do. But getting his hopes up about seeing his granddad again? Harrison had sounded positive on the phone when he'd called, but she knew how easy it was to get your hopes up and then have them come crashing down when something unexpected happened.

"Poppy?"

Hearing Alex say her first name made her smile. Earlier in the evening he'd still been calling her Ms. Carter. She gave him a tighter cuddle to let him know she'd heard him.

"You smell nice."

She dropped a kiss into his hair. Talk about a sweetie.

"And Poppy?"

"Yeah?"

"You're nice to snuggle. Just like what a mom would be like, I reckon."

Now she was struggling not to cry. Talk about a tug on her heartstrings....

"I think we should try to go to sleep now," she whispered, glancing at the clock. It was midnight already and she hadn't slept a wink. "Why don't we pull the covers up and close our eyes, okay?"

Alex nodded his head and tucked down, his little body warm against hers. With Katie tight on her other side, Poppy had never been so hot trying to go to sleep, but she'd never felt so loved, either. Felt as if she actually mattered. There was no pretending with kids, no ulterior motives. Katie and Alex had been comfortable enough to come into bed with her, had trusted that she cared for them and was going to help them.

And that was why she wanted to be a parent so badly. Why she still felt the pain of losing the baby she'd been so excited about carrying. When she'd reached the sixteen-week mark this time, she'd thought everything was okay, that nothing was going to go wrong again. She'd been so looking forward to finding out the gender, counting down the weeks until she'd know if she'd be buying pink clothes or blue, that losing her little baby hadn't even seemed a possibility.

The doctor had said it was the stress of everything, her body telling her it couldn't cope with nurturing a healthy baby and dealing with a divorce and losing all her money, too. Maybe it was a blessing in disguise, even if she couldn't see it now, especially after everything that had happened.

Poppy shut her eyes tight and focused on the pudgy hand pressed to her cheek, on the warm breath against her neck. Just because she wasn't going to be a mom anytime soon didn't mean she wasn't making a difference to the children in her life.

She blinked the tears away, refusing to get emotional.

But with these two in bed with her, she was starting to realize that it wasn't about having her own biological child. She'd just as happily parent these two for the sole reason that she was capable of loving them and they her.

But they already had a dad, and she had no idea what the situation was with their mom. *And she had no right to know.* She was their teacher and a friend of their father's. Thinking dangerous thoughts about how nice it would be to mean something more to them wasn't going to do her any favors.

What she needed to do was sleep. And forget about any fantasies she might have about being a parent, at least for a while. Because she couldn't be a mom without having a man in her life, and she wasn't even close to ready for that. Right now, she was meant to be harboring a grudge against the entire male population. No matter how nice she might think a certain Harrison Black was.

Because she'd thought Chris was nice, too, a man she could trust with her heart. And look how well that decision had turned out.

"I'm healthy. I'm a teacher. I make a difference," she whispered, forcing herself to practice her chant.

She shut her eyes and tried to focus on sleeping, counting every time she breathed in and exhaled.

If she wanted to stay in control, be in charge of her own destiny, then she just needed to take things one day at a time.

CHAPTER SEVEN

POPPY WAS EXHAUSTED. After hardly any sleep for two nights with the kids, then all day teaching, she was ready to drop. But she had two hungry children in the back of her car who were telling her all the things they wanted to show her when they got back to the ranch.

She crossed the almost-dry river, looking ahead to the house. It was beautiful—long and low, with a vine that grew across the front to soften the timber. *A home.* It looked like a home, not a house.

"It's Dad!"

Poppy's heart started to beat faster. Surely Harrison would have called if he was coming home early? "Where?"

"That's his truck," Katie told her, leaning forward. "Right there."

She pointed and Poppy saw where she was looking. It *was* Harrison. Or at least it was his truck, which meant he'd have to be around somewhere.

Oh, my God. She'd left her makeup and clothes in his bedroom, which meant that if he'd... She gulped. There was no point in worrying; they were both adults.

If he'd seen her underwear, it wasn't the worst thing in the world. Even if it felt like it right now.

"Where do you think he'll be?" she asked, trying to keep the alarm from her voice.

But the kids weren't listening to her, more interested in pressing their noses to the glass and searching for him. As soon as she stopped the car they were out, running as fast as they could to the house and racing through the front door.

Poppy took a moment to calm herself, to take some big, slow breaths and prepare herself for heading in. Because after the nights she'd had with his kids, the way she was feeling about them right now, she could easily think things about their dad that were forbidden; things she couldn't consider even if she wanted to.

He was sexy, he was single and he was…*not on her radar.* Or at least that's what she was trying to pretend.

She got out of the car, reached in for the slow-cooked beef pie she'd picked up at the bakery and walked as bravely as she could to the front door. Poppy could hear voices before she even stepped inside—mainly Harrison's deep, soothing tone.

It brought a smile to her face, because it sounded to her as if he was trying to explain that their granddad was okay and why he'd come home earlier than expected.

"Hi," she called out as she came into the kitchen. She didn't want to stand in the doorway listening without him knowing she was there. "I'm hoping you're back early because it's good news?"

Harrison gave her what looked like a relieved smile.

"It turns out he didn't even know he had dangerously high cholesterol, or if he did he certainly never told my mom, and he had a heart attack because of blocked arteries."

"But he's going to be okay?" she asked.

"He's going to need a decent period of rest and recovery, but yeah, he's going to be fine." Harrison grinned at his kids. "He told me to get back to these rascals, so I decided to come home."

They looked as relieved as he did, and she knew he'd been downplaying how distressed he'd been the other day for their sake. It was more than obvious that he loved his father, so the relief must have been enormous.

"Is he going to be kept in for long?"

"That's what I was just about to tell the kids," he said, looking from her to them. "I'm going to head back to the city, take them with me this time, then when he's ready I'll drive Dad home. Mom's a bit nervous, and we need to check in with the local doctor in Parkes on our way, too."

Poppy kept her smile plastered to her face, trying hard not to react. It was great that Harrison was taking his kids with him. She had no right to be sad about it.

"I've been trying to explain to them that Granddad had to have stents put in—"

"And it's gross," announced Katie, interrupting her dad and pulling a face.

"It might be gross but it saved your granddad's life," Harrison said, lifting her up to sit on the kitchen counter beside her brother.

"Did they put the stents through his arm?" Poppy asked.

Harrison nodded. "Yeah, they put dye through first because they were pretty blocked, then the stents. It was amazing." He raised his eyebrows, as if he'd just realized that she knew way too much about heart complications. "How did you know about stents, anyway?"

She shrugged, taking the pie over to the counter and placing it there before filling the jug with water for something to do. After the long day she'd had, she was ready for a coffee. A good, strong, black coffee.

"My dad had a heart attack, but he didn't make it. He had to have a triple bypass and there were complications."

Harrison gave her a tight smile. "I'm sorry. I know how lucky we are that Dad pulled through."

She shook her head. "Don't feel bad for telling me your dad made it, Harrison."

He planted his hands on the counter with a thump. The kids had gone quiet, listening to them talk, no doubt trying to understand what they were discussing. Poppy could tell he was trying to lift the mood, distract them.

"Coffee for everyone?" he asked.

"Dad! We don't drink coffee!" Katie squealed as he grabbed her around the waist and set her on her feet.

He did the same to Alex, only kept hold of him a little longer, giving the little guy a big hug. "Okay, so coffee for me and Poppy, and tea for you two."

Katie and Alex were both giggling now, jumping around like silly things.

"Fine, how about orange juice then?"

Poppy watched as he poured them each a glass before opening a container full of cookies and letting them take some.

"Why don't you guys have your snack outside and then play? We'll be out soon."

Poppy stayed silent and watched the kids go. They were such happy children, busy and lovable. Looking after them might have been tiring, but it certainly hadn't been hard.

"You do know what great children you have, right?"

He chuckled. "Yeah, I do. Although it's easy to think all kids are like that and forget how good mine are."

Now it was Poppy's turn to laugh. "Are you kidding me? I don't ever think all children are like that, and I've got *a lot* of experience in that department."

Harrison was staring at her, his body language different than it had been before. Around his children he was open and relaxed, but now that they were gone something had changed.

"I don't know how I'll ever thank you for looking after them for me," he said, pouring the coffee and sliding a mug across the counter toward her. "It meant a lot to me to get to the hospital when I did, and I'm glad they didn't see their granddad looking like that, all hooked up to machines and ghostly when I first got there."

Poppy knew exactly what he was talking about. "They were pretty upset the first night, worrying about him and wanting you, but we were fine. And they *are* great kids, I promise."

He took a sip of his coffee, but he was still staring at her.

"It wasn't until I started driving home today that I realized I'd never told you where anything was, or even which bed to sleep in," he said.

Poppy's face flushed hot and she hoped she wasn't blushing. "I, ah, hope you don't mind, but I slept in yours." *There, she'd said it.* Besides, he'd probably already been in there and noticed, anyway.

"Good. I didn't want you sleeping in the bunks, but I'm just sorry I didn't have time to put fresh sheets on."

She swallowed. Then swallowed again. She was glad he hadn't washed the sheets. His aftershave had been all over the pillows and she wasn't going to pretend she didn't appreciate the scent.

"It was fine, honestly. I'm just pleased I could help out," she said, trying to sound nonchalant when in reality her heart was beating overtime.

"Well, I left my things in the hall, anyway, just in case you had anything private in there."

Poppy's heart slowed then. Her embarrassment died faster than it had appeared. How the heck had she managed to meet a man with manners *this* good? Still, she was ready to change the subject.

"So when are you heading off? I hope you're not going to drive tired." The last thing she needed was to be worrying about him.

"Tomorrow," he said. "We'll leave tomorrow, so the kids will have at least a few days off school."

She shrugged. "No problem. Swing past if you want to take some reading or anything for them."

Poppy cradled her coffee and looked outside. She'd felt a lot of things around Harrison, but never awkward, which was exactly how she was feeling now.

Now? Now she didn't know what to say to him, how to look at him. Because she'd slept in his bed, cooked in his kitchen, cared for his children…and now it was *him* she was thinking about. What kissing him would be like, what touching him would be like, what letting something further develop between them would be like.

Stop! Poppy cleared her throat and just stood there, watching the children as they played outside. She was rebuilding her life here, on her own, to prove that she was capable of starting over. Men were not in her immediate future—not one-night stands, not relationships and certainly *not* Harrison Black.

"Poppy?"

He was standing behind her; she could feel it. Knew that he was too close, closer than he should be when they were nothing more than friends.

"Sometimes I think I could just stand for hours watching them," he said, voice low. "They're pretty good at leveling me when everything feels like it's turned to crap."

Poppy was still staring out the window, but she didn't know what to say, how to respond. But he was right. The way children could make you feel, the way they *did* make her feel, was one of the reasons she loved her job. Why she loved children.

Her body went rigid as metal. Harrison's hand had closed over her shoulder gently, as warm as if there was no fabric between them, even though there was.

She kept staring out the window even though she couldn't see anything, was blind to everything except his touch. Poppy wished she didn't feel this way, wished her resolve about men was stronger, but Harrison was the kind of man she'd wished she'd met all along. The kind of man that might be able to make her trust again, to make her love. And no matter how much her brain was telling her not to think that way, her heart was starting to tell her a different story altogether.

"Thank you, Poppy." His grasp changed then, becoming a soft squeeze that made her shut her eyes, trying to relax and summon enough courage to turn toward him. Because he still hadn't moved, which made her think he was waiting for her. "They've experienced a lot of heartache, a lot of pain over their mom leaving, even though they were so young when she left. It's not often I let someone close to them, so thank you for being there when they needed someone."

She pivoted slowly on the spot, and as she moved his hand fell away, brushing her hip as it skimmed past. But the rest of him seemed carved from stone—unmoving, unblinking, but not unseeing.

Harrison's gaze was steady, yet there was a seriousness in his stare that in equal parts thrilled and terrified her.

"I should go," she mumbled, her voice so quiet she wasn't even sure she'd spoken.

Harrison didn't say anything, but he did move. Now it was Poppy standing as if *she* was carved from stone, still as a statue as he slowly raised his hand, fingers brushing her jaw and staying there. When he pressed lightly, she moved into him, stepping into his space as if he'd asked her to.

Poppy ignored the warning voice in her head, switched it off and refused to be drawn away from something so magnetic, something she instinctively knew was going to feel good.

Harrison's mouth moved closer to hers, lips slightly parted, his eyes no longer looking into hers but staring at her mouth instead. His fingers were warm against her skin, sending tingles through her body that curled into her stomach, and his lips were hot.

Harrison kissed her so tenderly that she had to stifle a moan. She stood still, rooted to the spot, as though if she moved even an inch he might stop what he was doing and...

Oh. He didn't stop. Instead, he reached with his other hand to touch his fingers to the back of her skull, teased her even more with his mouth. Harrison's tongue softly, wetly tangled with hers, and still she didn't move, lost to the sensation of his lips against hers, in the most tender of embraces she'd ever experienced.

And then he pulled away—so slowly that she leaned forward, hungry to feel his mouth back on hers, to lose herself in the moment again.

But he put his hands on her arms then, holding her back, as if *she'd* been the one who'd started this in the first place.

"I don't know where that came from," he said, his voice a husky whisper.

Neither did she. But she did know that she'd liked it, even though her kissing Harrison had a voice in her mind screaming "No!" so loudly that it should have sent her running.

"Daddy!"

Katie's excited call made Poppy jump back a step, not wanting either of his children to catch them kissing. It was bad enough that she'd let it happen without having it complicate things for them, too.

Harrison cleared his throat. "In here, honey."

They were still staring at each other, not saying anything, and Poppy was alternating from having a million and one things to say to him to nothing at all.

"I think it's time for me to go," she murmured.

Harrison smiled, one side of his mouth kicking up at the corner. "You sure you don't want to stay for dinner?"

Did she ever. But she wasn't going to put herself through an evening with Harrison when what she needed was to establish distance between them. To set boundaries and follow through with them. To think about what had just happened.

"Harrison…" she began, not knowing how to say what she was feeling. Not *knowing* how she was actually feeling inside.

"Dad, we found a field mouse." Katie burst into the room. "Alex saw it, too."

Harrison kept watching Poppy, a beat too long, before turning his attention to his children. "How about you show me where you saw it," he said. "That'll give Poppy some time to get her things together."

Part of her liked that he was giving her some privacy, but another part? That part wanted him to ask her one more time to stay.

* * *

"Are you sure you won't stay for dinner?"

Poppy shook her head, but he could tell she'd considered it. The way she glanced around the room and looked at the kids told him she'd given it more thought than she was letting on.

"I really do need to go," she told him, slinging her overnight bag over her shoulder. "I don't want to drive back in the dark and Lucky will be missing me."

"Let me walk you out, then," he said, wanting a moment to talk to her alone before she left, because things were only going to get more awkward between them if he didn't bring up their kiss.

Why he'd needed to cross that boundary, when he had *zero* interest in taking things further with *any* woman, he didn't know. But he had, and now he needed to deal with the consequences.

"Honestly, I'm fine," she said, giving him a tight smile that he didn't buy for a moment. "Enjoy your trip to Sydney, kids."

They called out goodbye to her and Harrison followed Poppy to the front door, leaning past her to open it. She stayed still, as if she was too scared to touch him even by accident, until he stepped aside and she walked out to her car.

"Poppy, about before…" he started.

"You don't need to say anything, Harrison," she replied, not letting him finish.

He shoved his hands into his pockets, watched her as she threw her bag in the back and did everything to avoid making eye contact with him.

"It was a heat-of-the-moment thing and there's nothing to discuss," she said.

If there was nothing to discuss, then why was she trying to flee the scene so quickly?

"Poppy, I'm sorry," he said, needing to apologize before he managed to completely ruin their friendship. "I'm sure you're as hesitant as me to get, ah, *involved*." He paused, not wanting to dig himself a bigger hole than he had already. Nothing was coming out like he wanted it to. "What I mean is you're a beautiful, wonderful woman, but I didn't mean to give you the wrong idea."

She was looking even more embarrassed now than before he'd started to try and explain himself. *Crap!* He was making a complete hash of the entire situation.

"What I'm trying to say is that I got carried away before, but our friendship means a lot to me, and I'm so grateful for what you did, looking after the kids. I don't want to ruin that."

Poppy looked like a startled animal ready to flee, staring at him as if he'd announced he wanted to boil her cat and eat it.

"There's no need to apologize, Harrison," she finally said, breaking the silence. "It just happened, but I couldn't agree more. We're friends, and the last thing I'm interested in is something, well, something happening between us."

Harrison stood on the grass, wriggling his toes into it for something to do, and watched her get in her car.

"Thanks again for helping me out."

She nodded. "No problem. See you when you're back."

He pushed his hands even deeper into his jeans pockets and watched her drive off. Kind, sweet, beautiful Poppy, who he'd managed to thoroughly embarrass after she'd done so much for him. Then he'd talked rubbish, trying to explain his way out of what had happened.

But the problem wasn't what he'd done, it was how she'd responded. How they'd both responded. He'd meant to just touch her, then deliver a soft kiss, but the moment their lips had collided he'd been a goner, and if his daughter hadn't called out and broken the spell between them, he wasn't sure when he'd have pulled away.

Poppy was making him think things that weren't even a possibility for him or his children, not if he wanted to protect them, and it scared the hell out of him.

Harrison watched until her car disappeared from view, then went back inside. He had to heat the pie Poppy had left behind and slice it up for dinner, then pack their bags before they all went to bed. An early night was exactly what he needed before they made the drive back to Sydney. He wanted to leave early in the morning so the kids could just jump in the vehicle in their pajamas and fall back to sleep. That way, they'd make it to the city in time for lunch.

He also had to get on the phone and organize his workers, since he was going to be away for up to a week.

Poppy. Not seeing Poppy for a week? It was playing on his mind. He shrugged the thought away and slid the pie into the oven. Two weeks ago he hadn't even known her name and now he was acting as if he'd known her all his life.

So some time away? That might be just what he needed to get perspective again. Reset his boundaries; reaffirm them. Before he forgot all the reasons why he couldn't let a woman close to him. *Not ever again.*

CHAPTER EIGHT

POPPY SURVEYED THE garden and wondered where to start. She hadn't ever had a lawn to contend with before, or at least not since she was a little girl, and back then all she'd had to do was pretend she was mowing it. In fact, now that she thought about it, she recalled having a tiny pretend lawn mower that had blown bubbles.

The reality of mowing her own lawn wasn't so appealing, but it had to be done and she had nothing better to do.

Poppy looked at the old mower and sighed. She'd got it for nothing from one of her pupils' parents and she doubted it had been used for years. And her lawn looked as if it hadn't been cut in forever.

"Here goes," she muttered under her breath, pushing with all her might.

Five minutes later she was covered in sweat and the lawn looked as if it had been hacked by a machete. The only positive was that pushing the hell out of the mower had taken her mind off Harrison.

And now she was exhausted and thinking about him all over again.

She wanted to know why he'd kissed her, why he'd looked at her like that, why he was acting as if he wanted her one minute and then telling her why nothing could happen the next. She got it; she had to. Because if she was honest, she was the same, like a pendulum swinging hard one way, then zooming back in the other direction a second later. One moment she wanted Harrison to kiss her, to make her think that something could happen between them, and the next she was terrified by the idea of it. Thinking about what could go wrong, how he could hurt her, what had happened in the past... But deep down, she wanted to see if maybe she could make the right judgment call about a man. And whether that man *could* be Harrison.

The phone was ringing. She'd been so lost in her thoughts, and in surveying her stupid backyard, that she hadn't even noticed it bleating.

Poppy ran for the back door, scooted inside and grabbed the phone from its cradle.

"Hello?" She had no answering machine, and it drove her crazy to miss a call and not know who it was.

"Hey! It's me."

Poppy untwirled the cord and jumped up to sit on the counter. It was her sister. "You have no idea how much I needed to hear from you." She sighed down the line.

"You're not getting bored living out there in hick-ville, are you?"

"Do you have *any* idea how much I miss your teasing?"

They hadn't lived in the same place for years, but she was used to talking to her sister constantly—on the way to school when she'd been in the city, early in the evening, all the time.

"Tell me the goss. Any gorgeous single men?"

Poppy was pleased her sister couldn't see her smile. "You're not going to believe it, but yeah. There is."

Kelly screamed down the line. "I knew it! You little minx!"

Poppy twisted the cord around her finger, feeling like a teenager again just yapping to her sister on the old-fashioned phone. "I'm not interested in a relationship, Kelly. You know that."

She had a feeling that her sister would have slapped her if she'd been in the room. Especially if she'd seen the man they were talking about.

"Who says you need a relationship? Just have hot, steamy sex with him."

Poppy's face was suddenly on fire. Seriously, trust her sister to say something like that. "It's complicated," she started.

"How?"

"I teach his kids, and we've sort of become friends. And it's a really small town, did I mention that?" She was trying to think of every excuse possible, because now that she'd told her, Kelly was never going to back down.

"When are you seeing him next?"

Poppy sighed. "He's been out of town, but Mrs. Jones mentioned this morning that he'd been in to get his groceries."

"Think of an excuse and go see him. You know you deserve to be happy, right? *So be happy.* Not every guy is an asshole, Poppy, and if he is? Kick him straight to the curb."

Yeah, it was easy for her sister to say. She wasn't exactly the type to end up with the wool pulled over her eyes. Come to think of it, she probably tired of men before they had a chance to hurt her.

"He kind of lives a long way out, and I'm—"

"I said make up an excuse to see him, not make up an excuse to give me."

What could she say to that?

"Hey, I have to go. Call me tomorrow after you've seen him," Kelly said. "See ya."

Poppy hung up the phone and stayed seated on the counter, legs swinging. Lucky jumped up and joined her, looking out the window.

"Don't you dare laugh at the state of the grass," she ordered.

The truth was, she didn't care about the grass right now, because her sister had told her exactly what she'd been thinking anyway. And if they both had the same gut feeling...

What kind of excuse could she make to drive up to the ranch? To just turn up out of the blue? And what if she didn't want anything to happen between them?

She'd just come out of a long-term relationship, just dealt with her heart being broken. It wasn't that she didn't like Harrison, but...she wasn't a one-night stand kind of girl, either. And he'd made it perfectly clear that he wasn't interested in something permanent. So unless he changed his mind on that, she was going to have to forget all about him. But first she wanted to give him a chance.

* * *

Poppy was either making the biggest mistake or taking the best risk of her life. Given the intensity of the rain that was falling, she was starting to think it could be a sign, but then again, maybe she was just making excuses again.

The rain had come from nowhere, was bucketing down as if the sky was trying to punish them and her wipers were going flat tack.

It was a stupid plan. Who ever visited someone in this kind of weather? Although it hadn't been quite this bad when she'd made the decision to follow her sister's advice, so at least she had that as a backup excuse.

All she had come up with was something that was truthful, because she wasn't capable of lying or devising a fake reason to visit. It was the Aboriginal family she was going to see. And if she happened to end up spending time with Harrison, then so be it.

Katie had told her there were two children living on the ranch, probably a lot farther out, but still... She was the local teacher, and that meant she had an obligation to provide educational services to every child in the district.

Poppy squinted into the distance, sure she could see someone headed her way. Now that she'd hit the dirt road, she hadn't expected to encounter any other vehicles.

She slowed down, worried about visibility. The oncoming vehicle wasn't going too fast, but it flashed its lights at her. Was it Harrison?

It was. His black truck was almost beside her, and

she slowed even more. Now she felt like an idiot, and would likely end up mumbling a heap of nonsense when she came face-to-face with him. She'd come up with an excuse, but hadn't expected to have to explain herself before she even reached the ranch.

He stopped and wound down his window, and she did the same.

"Hi," she called out.

"What are you doing out here?" Harrison called back, his hair wet and plastered to his face.

She could see the kids in the back, and was embarrassed that she'd even come up with a plan at all just to see their dad. *Their gorgeous, wet, handsome-as-hell father.*

"It seems kind of crazy, given the weather, but I wanted to call in on the family you have living on the ranch. I'm told the children are homeschooled and I wanted to see if there's any way I can help them."

Harrison didn't question her, even though she knew her face was burning. She guessed he couldn't see the change in color through the rain.

"We've had a flash flood, and with the ground this dry our river's overflowing. Must be raining by the bucketload farther inland."

Yeah, really great timing on her part. "I'll come back another time," she said, wishing she'd never listened to her sister in the first place.

"You wouldn't be able to do me a huge favor, would you?"

"Sure." She was having to yell now, the rain was coming down so hard.

"I want to get the kids to my folks so I can deal with the storm and move the cattle to higher ground. But I'm running out of time before the water gets too high."

Poppy didn't need to be asked twice. "Get them in the back," she called to him. "I'll take them now."

"You sure?"

"Of course."

At least she could be helpful. Might take his mind off the fact she'd decided to make a house call to a remote ranch in weather like this. She'd never even thought about the riverbed leading to the property, that it could be flooded.

Harrison jumped out of his truck and grabbed Alex, putting him in the back of her car, then Katie.

"Hey, kids," she said.

They just grinned at her, a little shy from not having seen her all week.

"I owe you big time, *again*," Harrison said, standing out in the gale.

"It's fine. Just get out of the rain and head back home."

He called out some instructions to her, gave her his parents' address then turned around and drove toward the ranch.

Poppy took a deep breath before turning her car around, too. "So do you guys know where we're going?"

"Yes," said Katie. "It's really easy."

She grinned at the children in her rearview mirror, checking that their seat belts were done up.

So much for trying to seduce their father, if that's

what she'd actually been planning. She was much more capable of doing something with his kids.

They pulled up outside a sizable house not far from where Poppy lived. The town was small, so everything was relatively close, but they were on the outskirts and this house had to be the prettiest and nicest maintained of all the homes in Bellaroo Creek.

"This is their place?" she asked.

Katie nodded. "Yup."

Poppy pulled into the driveway, parking as close to the house as possible to avoid the kids getting too wet when they got out. "Okay, let's go," she told them, grabbing their overnight bag from the passenger seat and leaping out of the car.

The front door was open before they even reached the porch. An older, attractive woman was waiting for them, her hair pulled back into a bun, gray but immaculate.

"In you scoot," she said, smiling at the children as they ran past her into the house. "And you must be Ms. Carter."

Poppy held out her hand. "To the children, yes. I'm Poppy."

"Nice to finally meet you after hearing so much about you this past week."

Hearing so much about her? "I hope it was only good things." What else could she say in response to that?

"Of course. Now, dear, I'd ask you in, but my son's

just phoned with a bit of an emergency. He wanted me to go, but…" The other woman sighed.

Poppy's heart sank. "Is he okay?" Surely his mom wouldn't be standing making small talk with her if something terrible had happened?

"Are you any good at delivering babies?"

What? "Um, I can't say I have any experience *delivering* babies, exactly, but I was my best friend's birthing partner when she had both her children."

"Thank goodness." Harrison's mom reached out and touched her forearm. "Did Harrison ever mention the family living in one of the workers' homes?"

Poppy refused to blush, even though her entire plan about seeing Harrison had revolved around the family they were talking about. "Yes, it's why I was heading to the ranch today. To see them." She was getting a lot better at delivering her line.

"Well, she's gone into labor a few weeks early, and Harrison's all in a flap, worried about her, even though I know for a fact her husband delivered her other two at home with no problems."

"So you're asking *me* to go back and assist with the labor?" Poppy took a deep breath. "I mean, well…" She paused. What the hell did she mean? The woman was in the middle of nowhere during a storm, which meant she had no other choice *but* to be capable.

"He said he'd meet me near the river, but I'm sure he'll be pleased to see you instead. He'll take you over the flooding in the helicopter."

This was actually happening. She had a legitimate reason to see him, to spend time with him, and she was so nervous her legs were in danger of buckling beneath her.

"I guess this is another good way to become part of the community, right?" she managed to reply, trying not to let on how nervous she was. So much for the afternoon with Harrison that she'd hoped for.

"That's a girl. Now get in that car and drive safely."

Poppy was numb, but she smiled and walked back to the car. The only consolation was that she got to see Harrison again.

CHAPTER NINE

HARRISON HOVERED THE helicopter, going closer to the car than he had intended but needing to force her to stop. The weather conditions weren't great, but he'd been up in worse and right now his primary concern was ensuring he didn't put Poppy's life in danger by letting her get too close to the river. He was guessing she'd offered to take his mom's place in coming—either that or his mother had seen it as an opportunity to matchmake.

He watched as Poppy stopped the vehicle but she didn't get out straightaway and he wasn't sure if she could see him waving to her or not. Even though the rain was still pelting from the sky he decided to touch down, because the wind had died off and it was probably safest.

Harrison jumped from the chopper once it was clear and ran toward Poppy. She climbed out of the vehicle when she saw him, coat held above her head, and he put his arm around her as they ran back. There was no point trying to talk until they were inside the helicopter.

He opened her door, helped her up then ran around

to his side, hauling himself up, shutting the door and turning to her.

"Hell of a way we keep meeting," he joked, pleased to see a smile on her face even though she was drenched.

"I'm trying to convince myself this whole situation is character building," she told him. "That's the kind of thing I'd tell my pupils, anyway."

Harrison leaned over and helped her with the cross-over seat belt, then passed her a headset. "Put this on. I have to get this bird up now while it's safe, and we can keep talking through these." He put his own on, then ignored everything else while he flicked switches and put them up in the air. He knew better than to let anything distract him when there was no margin for error.

"I'll take us close to the barn," he told her as they went up and across the river. "My truck's parked there."

"Oh my goodness, oh my goodness."

Harrison glanced at her. "Are you okay?" The last thing he needed was her freaking out before they touched down. "We'll be grounded in less than a minute."

"I'll be fine," she said, although her voice was wobbly. Even through the headset he could hear how panicked she was. "Just…" She didn't finish her sentence.

"This river is usually dry through this part of the year, but the heavy rainfall farther inland has pushed a lot of water down. The ground's really dry right now, which is why it floods so quickly." He was trying to soothe her, to take her mind off her worries. He loved being in the air, but knew plenty of people were terrified of flying. Especially in a helicopter. "Over winter we're flooded in for a good few weeks sometimes, would you believe?"

She wasn't saying anything now, but he was hoping that listening to him had taken her mind off her fears.

"Here we go, ready to land already."

Harrison brought the chopper down as steadily as he could, even though the rain lashing against them and the wind picking up again wasn't making it easy. One of his ranch hands was waiting for them, running out, head tucked low, to assist. Harrison jumped out as soon as it was safe and went around to help Poppy out, holding her hand and running with her to his truck.

"Give me a minute, okay?"

He didn't wait for her reply but bolted back to the helicopter as fast as he could, securing the rotors down with ropes they had at the ready and manhandling the cover over the cockpit.

"Thanks, Chad," he called out.

His young ranch hand was soaked to the bone—they'd all been out far too long in the wet weather already—but he was jogging back over to him.

"Hey, boss, Sally's had her baby. Arrived while you were gone, and Rocky called it through on the sat phone."

Harrison indicated for him to join him in the barn. "She's had it? Already?"

"Yeah, Rocky went straight back to the cottage, just like you told him to, and he called to say it was their fastest baby yet."

"And they've got everything under control? They

don't need any help with…" he paused, running a hand through his wet hair "…I don't know, women's stuff?"

"Yeah, he said they're all good. Said he'd call you if they needed your mom." The young man laughed. "Although I can see it's actually your *lady friend* come to help."

Harrison glared at him, raising an eyebrow. "She's not my *lady friend*, Chad. She's the kids' teacher."

He received another laugh in response and he shook his head. Clearly he'd been way too lenient with his young worker for him to tease him like that, *especially* about a woman.

"Whatever you say, boss."

Harrison started to walk off, then spun around again. "What did they have?"

"Little girl," Chad called out, walking backward through the barn.

"Hey, you guys may as well call it a day. Warm up and dry off before you catch a cold. And don't forget to feed the dogs."

Harrison put his head down and ran for the vehicle. Now that the baby was safely delivered, there was no reason for Poppy to be here. But he had no intention of taking the helicopter up again, and the river was way too high to cross even in his truck.

Which meant Poppy was stranded here for the night with him.

He could see her sitting inside, watching him, until he yanked the door open and jumped in. "I have good news," he said, smiling. Or at least he hoped she thought being stuck with him, and not having to help bring a baby into the world, was what she'd consider good news.

All Poppy could think about was how reckless she was being, listening to her heart instead of her head. Either reckless or stupid. She couldn't decide which.

The fact that, instead of looking pretty and serene, she was soaking wet and freezing cold, was running through her mind, too. She was stuck at Harrison's ranch until she didn't have a clue when, which meant she needed to get over her embarrassment at being here and looking like a drowned rat. Or at least start to believe the lie she was stating—that she'd headed in the direction of the ranch to see the family. The family whose baby she was also meant to have helped deliver.

Arghh. Nothing about today had turned out as planned.

"So how's your dad doing?" she asked, unable to think of anything else to say.

"Great. He's doing great," Harrison replied.

They stayed silent again, as if he was as troubled for words as she was.

"I'll pull up right against the house," he told her. "Although given how wet we are—" he looked at her and then down at himself "—I'm not sure it's going to help any."

Poppy hadn't dared to look at herself in the mirror, even while she'd been in the vehicle alone, because there wasn't much she could do. Except perhaps rub any smudged mascara from beneath her eyes.

"Okay, run whenever you're ready. Just don't slip on the brickwork."

If he hadn't warned her, she probably would have done exactly that.

Poppy moved quickly up the steps and into the shelter of the porch and Harrison was right behind her. His body knocked hers, pressing into her for a second before he slid back out of the way.

"Sorry," he said, pushing the door. "It's not locked. I don't think anyone would bother to burgle us."

She laughed, but it came out all nervous sounding. She seriously needed to get a grip. Poppy focused on walking into the house, waiting for Harrison to flick on the lights, before realizing she was making a puddle on the floor. Thank goodness she'd had a coat on to keep her top relatively dry, but her lower legs were soaked and she sure wasn't going to strip off her pants.

"I'm making your floor all wet."

"Ditto." Harrison laughed, but at least he had wet-weather gear on. "I'm going to hit the shower and change clothes. Is there anything I can get you? You know where the main bathroom is if you want to grab a shower, too."

She shook her head. "No, I'm good. I'll just…" What? She wasn't exactly sure what she was going to do. "You go have a shower and I'll try to dry off."

Poppy watched as he peeled off his jacket, sweater and socks, rolled up the bottoms of his jeans then crossed the room and disappeared.

"I'll crank up the fire, make it warmer in here," he called out.

Hopefully, it would warm enough for her to dry out quickly, because she wanted to take as few clothes off as possible. She stood, listening to him putting logs on the fire, hearing the flames hiss, then his footfalls as he walked to his bathroom. She stripped off her shoes and socks, removed her sweater and carried them all into the living room. Water was still dripping from her jeans, so she rolled up the denim.

At least she had her handbag, although it held only tissues, lip gloss and some mascara. Maybe some old mints, too, if she was lucky, but probably not much else.

On second thought, maybe she should use the bathroom. She could tidy up a little, try to wring some of the water from her jeans and make sure her tank top wasn't indecently tight. Not that she had any other options if it was, given that she'd never planned on anyone seeing it.

If her mobile phone worked out here, she could have called her sister for a pep talk, a confidence boost, but technology wasn't her friend in Bellaroo.

She heard the pipes groan and then go silent. Which meant Harrison was out of the shower.

It also meant she didn't have long before she had to face him...for the rest of the night.

Harrison could hear Poppy in the living room. He pulled his shirt on and started walking, finding her standing in front of the fire and looking at some photographs on the mantel.

"Warming up?"

"Yeah," she replied, turning to face him.

She was beautiful; he couldn't deny it, even if he was trying to stop thinking about her like that. After their kiss...

He pushed the thought away. It didn't matter how much he liked her; it wasn't a possibility. Which meant he had to treat her like the friend she was and nothing else.

"Is this your wife?" she asked.

"Ex," he snapped, instantly wishing he hadn't answered quite so quickly or with such a bitter tone.

"She's beautiful," Poppy said, still staring at the photo. "And it's nice that you keep a photo here after, well, you know. I'm sure it was difficult."

Yeah, he knew. "It's not the kids' fault that she left, but she still brought them into this world." He paused, watching Poppy. "I'll never understand how she did it, but now when I think about it, I'd like to believe she wanted to give them a better life. That maybe she did it for them, because she couldn't be the mom she thought they deserved."

Poppy was staring at him now, the photo forgotten. "I know it's not my place to say anything, but I just don't get how a woman can leave her kids. I mean, to completely walk out on your own flesh and blood seems..."

"Cold?" he finished for her. "Cruel, unbelievable?"

Her expression was sad. "Exactly."

A moment earlier he'd been feeling exhausted but happy. Now he was just annoyed that they'd somehow ended up talking about his past when for once he'd forgotten about it.

"When I said to you the other day that I wasn't ready for anything, that I couldn't take what I started with you any further," he told her, forcing himself to meet her eye, "*that's* why. Because I don't trust that someone else won't hurt my children again. No matter who that person is. And that means I can't let anyone into my life. It's why I'm so protective."

Poppy sighed. He couldn't read her expression, but he could tell she disagreed with him about something.

"Believe me, I have trust issues, too. But maybe we have to move forward in order to let go."

No, she was wrong. "Or maybe we have to hold on to it," he said, anger starting to thump through his body. "Instead of making the same mistake all over again."

CHAPTER TEN

"I'M NOT YOUR ex-wife, Harrison, so you don't need to speak to me like I am."

He glared at her, so angry she could feel it. His jaw was clamped so tight she could see a flicker in his cheek.

"You have no idea what you're talking about," he growled. "I'm trying to be honest with you, not pretend that you're *her*, but you don't seem to get the reality of what happened."

Now it was Poppy's turn to glare, to be furious with him, because she *did* get it, and it was about time he listened to her.

"I know that she left you, and I know that you've raised your children alone. If you want to elaborate, then by all means," she said, refusing to raise her voice. He could get as angry and loud as he liked, but she was not going to get into a yelling match with him, any more than she was going to let him speak to her like that. "All I'm saying is—"

"My wife left me as if our marriage vows meant nothing," he interrupted, his voice a low hiss. "I don't care that she left me, but I do care that she left our children. Don't get me wrong, I cared plenty at the time, but seeing the pain in their faces, seeing the confusion in their eyes when I had to explain to them why she didn't want anything to do with them anymore… It doesn't matter that I've made peace with raising them on my own because they'll never understand what she did." Harrison shook his head and strode away before turning and pacing straight back in Poppy's direction. "How do you think your husband feels? Did you just walk out on him, too? What would he think if he knew…" Harrison's voice trailed off.

How dare he turn the conversation around like that and try to make *her* into a villain? This was about him, not her.

"If he knew what?" she asked, knowing full well what he was going to say.

"If he knew that you'd been unfaithful? That we'd kissed?"

She laughed—a weird, evil laugh that she'd never heard come from her own mouth before. "You think *I've* been unfaithful?" Oh, if only he knew the half of it.

Harrison was staring at her hard, his eyes never leaving hers, almost as if he was trying to set her on fire with his gaze. She had no idea why he was taking so much of his anger out on her, why he'd somehow made all this *her* fault.

"Unfaithful is finding your husband in bed with another woman," she said, refusing to back down now she'd started, not prepared to let him think that what had happened to her was *her* fault. Not when she'd finally managed to believe the truth herself. "Sorry, in *my* bed," she corrected. "Naked and in bed with another woman, and only discovered because I decided not to stay late and mark term papers but went home instead. So if you wanted to hear about *unfaithful*, now you have."

The look on Harrison's face had changed. Gone was the anger, the wildness in his eyes that had taken over his entire expression only a minute earlier. But he'd asked. He'd accused her of being, what? An *adulteress*? Just because she hadn't received her divorce papers in the mail yet?

"My marriage is over, Harrison. And you'll find that it was my husband's choice to ruin things between us, not mine."

Poppy watched as he swallowed, almost enjoying how uncomfortable he looked after the way he'd spoken to her.

"Poppy, I'm sorry. I never should have said anything when I had no idea what you'd been through." His voice was deep, commanding.

She shrugged. "Your wife hurt you, *badly*. I get that. But it doesn't mean that every other woman who walks away from a marriage is at fault."

Harrison stood so still he seemed to be carved from marble, a statue in the room facing her.

"My husband not only cheated on me, Harrison, he took everything from me."

"I don't understand."

Poppy looked up at the light, staring at it, forcing her emotion away. Refusing to succumb to the tears that were threatening, so close to the surface she didn't know if she had the strength to fight them.

"I've worked so hard all my life to have somewhere nice to live, to afford the little luxuries I wanted, and when my dad passed away, he left me half of everything he owned. My sister and I received equal shares of his estate, and I didn't waste a cent because I know how hard he had worked for everything he had."

Harrison just stared at her, but now his gaze was soft and caring, as if he was feeling every flash of the pain that was going through her body and truly regretted his burst of anger.

"I'd been with my husband for years, had known him since we were at school together, and I'd never known he was a gambler," she confessed, ready to tell Harrison everything. "It turns out that he'd slowly been getting us further and further into debt without me knowing. And because we owned everything together—" Poppy shrugged and took a deep breath "—he managed to lose our house, our cars, *everything*. He'd drained my bank account without me even knowing, all because I'd trusted him too much."

"Oh, Poppy, I'm so sorry."

She bravely tilted her chin up, blinked the tears away again and held her head high. "So that's why I'm here, trying to start over and forget the last year even existed."

"I never should have been so hard on you. I'm sorry, I..." Harrison looked torn, as if he didn't know what to say or how to go about comforting her.

Poppy squared her shoulders. "So now you know all

my dirty secrets," she said. "I'm an almost-divorcee, I'm broke and I managed to spend all my married years not knowing my husband was screwing around behind my back, with my money and the woman who lived across the hall from us."

"I guess we have more in common than we realized," Harrison said, his voice soft now, which seemed to soothe the thumping of her head and the shaking of her hands.

"Yeah," she muttered, crossing her arms.

But it was too late. Harrison had already seen her hands shaking and he was stepping forward and reaching for them, interlacing their fingers.

"You know what I'm wondering?" he asked, pulling her so slowly toward him that her body obeyed without her consent.

"What?" she whispered, staring at his hands instead of his face.

"How any man could ask another woman to his bed when he already had you to come home to."

Poppy didn't believe him, not for a moment, but his words still put a smile on her face. "I don't believe you, but thanks," she said, braving his gaze and wishing she hadn't, staring at him now as if she was stuck in the web of his eyes, hypnotized, with no chance of reprieve.

"If you don't believe me, then how about I show you?" Harrison's voice was so low, so husky, that she was powerless to resist him.

His hand left hers and slowly reached for her face, his palm cupping her cheek, fingers tucking beneath her chin and raising it. Poppy complied, more because she couldn't *not* than because she consented.

Harrison dipped his head, eyes dropping to her mouth, and she did the same. Because his lips were moving toward hers and she wasn't going to pull away.

His mouth was inches from hers, his breath warm against her skin, but still he hesitated, as if waiting for her to accept, to make the final decision.

Hell, yes. The words ran through her mind at the same time as she stepped toward him, just one step, but enough for their bodies to touch and their lips to meet in a kiss that stole her breath away and made her arms snake around the back of his neck. Her fingers found their way into his hair as his hands enclosed her waist, holding her still as their mouths danced, as his tongue so gently played against hers.

So what if she'd promised to stay away from men? Harrison Black had been on her mind since her first day in town, and if she didn't get this out of her system now, then she'd probably never get a good night's sleep ever again. Besides, maybe she didn't need long-term. Maybe one night was enough.

Maybe he'd gone mad. It was the only reason to explain why his lips were currently locked on Poppy's and why he wasn't capable of pulling away even if he'd wanted to.

Her mouth was soft yet firm against his, her hips pulled in tight to his stomach, and he couldn't keep his hands off her. They were skimming her waist, touching her hips, running down the curve of her—

"Stop." Poppy's voice was breathless, but his hands froze at the same time his lips did.

She said *stop*, he stopped. No questions asked. But…

"You okay?" he managed to rasp.

Poppy was nodding, as if trying to convince herself that she *was* okay. "It's just…" Her sentence trailed off and she touched her fingers to her mouth, as if remembering what they'd been doing, touching where *his* lips had been. "I'm not sure… I mean, I don't know if I'm ready for this."

"Poppy, I don't know if either of us is ready for this, not mentally," he said, inching closer again, reaching out slowly to touch her arm. But he was sure ready *physically.*

"Then why are we doing this?" she asked, her eyes connecting with his.

"Because it feels so good?"

Harrison was smiling; he couldn't help it. Because it was the truth. Did he want to be with another woman again, theoretically? *No.* But the pull he'd felt toward Poppy, the amount of time he was spending thinking about her? That was telling him he didn't really have a choice. If they kissed, they kissed, and he'd have to deal with the consequences later.

Poppy was grinning now, and he started to laugh. She did, too.

"How did we end up here?" she asked him, stepping into his arms and dropping her head to his shoulder.

"I have no idea," he replied truthfully, pressing a kiss into her hair.

"How about something to eat?" she murmured.

Harrison took a deep breath, then blew it out slowly. "Sure, why not."

Eating wasn't exactly what he'd had on his mind, but what else were they going to do? For now, the power hadn't gone out, but they were stuck, and would be at least until morning.

So he needed to get his head straight, forget about what had happened and go back to thinking of Poppy as a friend.

She stepped out of his embrace and made for the kitchen, and he couldn't take his eyes from her body. Her sweater was slung over the back of a chair, damp from the rain earlier, so she was just in her jeans and a skintight tank top. Everything clung to her body, showing off every single curve she possessed.

Harrison groaned. It was time he started being honest with himself, and the first step was admitting that he'd never, ever thought of Poppy as just a friend.

In the beginning, she'd infuriated him because he'd needed someone to be angry at and she'd given him a tongue-lashing for being rude. Ever since then he'd been fighting something else entirely, and tonight, if he'd had his way, he'd be giving in to those desires in a heartbeat.

"Are you coming?" Poppy called.

Harrison marched out to the kitchen after her. Food was better than nothing, and she was a pretty good cook.

CHAPTER ELEVEN

POPPY WAS TRYING hard to concentrate on dinner, but it wasn't easy. She could feel Harrison watching her, knew he was staring at her, tracking her every move, and it was making her feel...nervous. This man— this gorgeous, sexy-as-hell man whose house she was stranded in, and who she'd pulled away from earlier when all she'd wanted was to kiss him over and over again—was so tempting it was killing her. And the more she thought about how she'd pushed him away, the more she wanted him. Even though it went against everything she'd vowed not to do.

"Where did you learn to cook like this?" he asked.

"I love being in the kitchen, and I was pretty addicted to the food channel for a while." It was true; sometimes she'd preferred to stay home, glued to the television. Although in hindsight, she might have been more sensible keeping an eye on her husband. "But don't get too excited, it's just a French omelet. I know you can do better."

"Well, it smells fantastic. I can only cook Thai, remember?"

A sudden loud bang sent her sky-high, dropping the pan with a crash to the counter.

"Crap!" Poppy's hand was heating up already from where the pan had burned her, but she couldn't see anything. The lights had gone out, leaving them bathed in darkness. A complete blackout.

"It's okay," Harrison reassured her.

She could hear him but couldn't see him, and she was starting to panic. She was used to having streetlights, not this kind of midnight dark.

"Just wait for a minute until your eyes adjust," he said. "There's a flashlight in the top drawer and I've got one at the back door."

"What the hell just happened?"

"The storm has killed the power. Must have been a fuse blowing to make that kind of bang. I'm going out to check it, so you sit tight."

The last thing she wanted was to be left alone, but Harrison was right. Her eyes were slowly starting to adjust, enough for her to shuffle to the top drawer and find the flashlight. She flicked it on, took a deep breath and held the light to her hand. It was only a tiny patch on her finger that had burned, but it was stinging and she wanted to get it under cold water. At least doing that might take her mind off the fact that she was starting to feel like they were in a horror movie.

Poppy pushed the pan away from the edge of the counter and held her finger under the faucet, shivering as the cold water touched her skin.

"We've definitely lost power."

She turned at the sound of Harrison's voice, making out his silhouette, then seeing him more clearly as he came closer.

"So we're stuck in the dark for the whole night?" she asked.

She didn't know whether it was not having any power or lights or the fact that she was stranded with a man who in equal parts terrified and excited her, but her skin was covered in goose pimples, and not just from the cold water.

"This kind of thing happens out here more often than you'd think, so we're prepared." Harrison walked into the kitchen like a man on a mission, but he stopped dead when he saw her with her finger immersed in the water. "What happened?"

"Burned myself when the lights went out," she told him.

Harrison put down whatever it was he was carrying and turned the faucet off. He held her finger up to the light and inspected it, so tenderly she could scarcely feel his touch.

"How badly does it hurt?" he asked.

"I've had it under water this whole time. It's no big deal." She couldn't even feel the pain any longer. Although that probably had more to do with the proximity of the man standing in front of her than anything else.

"Poppy?"

The way Harrison said her name made the blood pump through her veins as fast as if she'd just finished a marathon. He'd said it as a question, as if he wanted something from her, only she wasn't sure quite what he wanted, and all sorts of thoughts were racing through her mind.

But he didn't bother saying anything else.

Instead, Harrison closed the gap between them and grabbed the back of her head, fisting his hand in her hair and kissing her so hard she could hardly breathe. But she had no intention of resisting, was powerless to.

He grabbed her around the waist without breaking their kiss, hoisting her up onto the counter and pushing his body between her legs. His face was damp, his hair wet from being out in the rain, but she didn't care.

Instead, she obliged. Poppy tucked her legs around his waist, keeping him close and holding on to his shoulders, running her hands down his back and letting her fingers explore his muscles, the curve of his shoulder blades, the back of his arms.

"Are you sure this time?" He'd pulled back just enough to murmur against her lips, was kissing her again before she had time to answer.

Poppy tried to nod, but it was useless, and she was so focused on his tongue against hers, on the way his lips were moving softly one moment, then roughly the next, that she couldn't even comprehend talking.

Because that would involve putting distance between them, and she didn't want that. Not at all. What she wanted was for Harrison to kiss her and kiss her until that was all she could remember.

A crash outside sent her leaping off the counter and into his arms, legs knotted tightly around his waist.

"What was that?"

The storm was raging, with rain teeming down so

hard now she figured it was a wonder water wasn't pouring through the roof.

"Just a tree," he said, trailing gentle kisses down her neck while her attention was diverted. His arms cupped beneath her bottom, held her locked in place.

Poppy sighed and tried to relax again, giggling when he nibbled the edge of her collarbone.

"It doesn't matter what's out there, Poppy," he murmured in between kisses, plucking at her skin so softly that she didn't even realize he'd sat her back down on the counter. "I'll protect you."

She shut her eyes and tipped her head back, the touch of his mouth on her neck and chest enough to make her moan. But she knew he was telling the truth.

Whatever his downfalls were, he would protect her, no matter what. She'd seen firsthand how much he loved his children, had witnessed his strength and determination, and that told her she was safe. That he'd do whatever it took to protect her in the truest sense of the word.

"I think," he whispered against her skin, gently inclining her head forward so he could find his way back to her lips, "that we should take this somewhere more comfortable."

Poppy slid her arms around his neck. That sounded like a very, very good idea.

So much for staying strong and resisting her. Harrison carried Poppy to the fire, gently placing her on the big leather sofa in front of it. The room was almost dark, the red glow from the flames casting a low light and creating shadows.

"I still can't believe I'm stranded here."

Harrison smiled down at Poppy, sitting on the edge of the sofa as she snuggled back into the cushions. "If I didn't know better I might think you'd planned it."

"Yeah, I called on Zeus for some help up there in the sky, and he had someone cut the power," she said sarcastically.

Harrison lay down alongside her, length to length, their bodies just touching. He watched as Poppy sucked part of her bottom lip between her teeth, her eyes dancing from his lips to his eyes and back again.

Wow, she was sexy.

"Hey," he whispered, reaching out to touch her face, smoothing a few loose strands of hair back before trailing a finger down her jawline.

She giggled. It was so soft and unexpected it made him chuckle in turn.

"A few years ago I promised myself never to let a woman into my heart or my home ever again," he told her. It was the truth, but he'd never told anyone, never shared how determined he'd been not to be hurt again or experience what it was like to lose all faith in another human being and be prepared to do anything to protect his children.

"Sounds kind of familiar to me," she replied in a low voice. "I came here because I thought it'd be country hicks and old guys."

Harrison gave her a soft punch to the arm. "Who are you calling a hick?"

She shook her head and sucked in her bottom lip

again as she stared straight into his eyes. "Not you," she said.

Poppy barely moved, just the smallest wriggle of her hips, but it was enough to press their bodies more tightly together, for the tip of her nose to be touching his, for her mouth to be so near that he couldn't think of anything other than kissing her. Again. And again.

Screw it. Why was he holding back? When there was a beautiful woman lying beside him, telling him with every bit of her body language that she wanted him as badly as he wanted her?

Harrison skimmed his fingers along her side, down her torso and to her thigh, at the same time as he brought his lips closer to hers. He tasted her mouth, their lips meeting, tongues colliding so delicately that it made her moan. And when she moaned, she thrust her body tighter to his, one hand gripping his shirt as if she was holding him in place, refusing to let him move, taking charge.

He hadn't been with a woman in…way too long. Had tried to pretend that he was fine on his own as a bachelor, that he didn't need the comfort of a woman. But Poppy? She was telling his body an entirely different story.

She was warm and soft against him, her touch gentle. Poppy's mouth was yielding to his, but the way she was holding on to him told him he was a fool to think he was the one in control here. And he didn't care. Not one bit.

But he was scared. Scared that he'd let a woman into his home, into his life. Because the only women he'd been with since his wife left had been one-night stands when he'd been in the city. Poppy? Poppy was no one-night stand.

She held his face between her hands now and had flipped so she was sitting astride him. Harrison couldn't think, not about *anything* other than the woman looking down at him. She'd broken their kiss, but was leaning forward again, her long hair falling over one shoulder and curling on his chest, her full lips kissing his jaw, then the side of his mouth, before he grabbed hold of her arms, forced his lips to hers.

Poppy kissed him over and over, and he complied, lost to everything except the way her body felt in his hands, the flash of her aqua eyes as they met his every so often before shutting again, as if she was as lost to pleasure as he was.

Harrison couldn't take it any longer. He needed to touch her skin, to see her bare, and he wasn't going to wait.

He pushed her top up, smiling when she sat back and finished the task, tugging it over her head and throwing it to the ground. Her bra was black, plain but pretty, and he wanted it off.

"No," she whispered, when he went to unhook it. Poppy was shaking her head, so he stopped, not wanting to push her.

"Why?" he asked, needing to know. "You don't have to be embarrassed, Poppy. You're beautiful."

She had a wicked look on her face, a grin that told him she was feeling more confident that he'd realized. The light flickering from the fire was making her blond hair into a golden haze, an ethereal effect that left him wondering if he wasn't dreaming about having his children's teacher poised above him in her bra.

"You first," she whispered, wriggling down his legs and pushing his T-shirt up. Her tongue followed her fingers, trailing across his skin. He could hardly stay still. It was torture.

"You're the devil, you know that?" He sucked back a breath as she nipped at his belly with her teeth.

Harrison yanked his T-shirt off and flung it away before grabbing Poppy and flipping her so she was beneath him.

"Hey!" she protested.

"You *are* the devil," he whispered, teasing her the same way she'd teased him, but holding her down by the wrists so she couldn't squirm away even if she tried. *"And I like it."*

Poppy had no idea where her confidence was coming from, but she wasn't going to waste time questioning it. She'd been terrified at the thought of being with another man after so long with her husband, but she needn't have worried. Because Harrison was so kind, so sexy, so *consuming* that she wasn't even having time to worry.

"Off," he ordered, fiddling with the top button of her jeans, lifting his weight just enough to pull them down, but not enough to let her escape.

Poppy tugged at her pants until they were around her ankles so she could kick them free, watching as he did the same, sitting up and discarding his until they were both clothed in only their underwear.

This was actually happening. She sucked back a breath as he lowered himself over her again, with care this time, so unlike before when he'd flipped her and pinned her down. Now he was back to being careful with her, to touching her as if she was so delicate she was in danger of breaking.

"You sure about this?" Harrison's voice was gruff, so unlike his usual tone.

Poppy nodded. "I'm sure." And she was. Nervous, definitely; hesitant, yes. But there was no part of her that didn't want Harrison. And she wasn't going to let a sudden jangle of nerves get in the way of her enjoying herself.

They were stranded at his ranch house, in the dark, and she was lying in the arms of a man who could literally steal her breath away with one touch or kiss. So she was *not* going to back down now.

Harrison was staring into her eyes, waiting for her. As if he wasn't convinced.

So she showed him. Poppy reached behind her and flicked the hooks on her bra, shrugging out of it so she was lying there bare. Harrison's eyes flashed brightly as they stared from her breasts to her eyes and back again.

She reached for him, cupped the back of his head and drew him closer until his warm chest was pressed against her skin, firm against her breasts.

Then she kissed him, lightly at first, teasing him, then pulling him harder against her, her mouth firm against his. His lips touching hers sent licks of heat through her body, and his hand reaching to cover her breast, the roughness of his skin against the softness of hers, was making her think all kinds of wild thoughts.

If she was going to break her promise to herself, she was glad she was breaking it with Harrison.

"Thank you," she whispered.

"For what?" he murmured, pulling back to look at her.

"For making me feel wanted again."

Harrison grinned and snapped the elastic of her panties, making her squeal. "Baby, I couldn't want you any more if I tried."

CHAPTER TWELVE

POPPY OPENED HER eyes, blinking until the blur cleared. She snuggled deeper beneath the blanket, tucked so tightly against Harrison that they may as well have been one.

The light from the fire was orange now, the flames dull compared to their earlier brightness, but the room was still warm and she wasn't going to get up and throw more wood on. She'd never been in a house with a real fire before, but there was something soothing about watching flames lick against wood. Even the smell of the timber burning was kind of comforting.

"Hey, beautiful." Harrison was stretching out one arm, the other still pinned beneath her. "What time is it?"

She had no idea, so she just shook her head, then leaned toward him and placed a soft kiss to his lips before wriggling down a little to press her face into his chest. There was no way she wanted to get up, no matter what the time was.

"This," he said, dropping a kiss into her hair, "is a nice way to wake up."

"Uh-huh," she murmured, not letting go of him.

"The rain sounds like it's stopped, too," Harrison said.

They lay there in silence, the early-morning light starting to filter in.

"Will the power still be out? I'd offer to make pancakes or French toast, but I can't do much without power." Her stomach was rumbling so loudly that it was going to embarrass her if she didn't eat something soon. "I can't believe we didn't eat dinner, when I had it almost ready."

"Poppy, there's something I need to tell you."

She groaned. "If you have a deep, dark confession to make, it's a little late."

Harrison tugged her up so they were lying nose to nose. His body was still pressed to hers, legs tangled beneath the blanket.

"It's nothing terrible, but I think you'll be angry with me."

What was he talking about? "Harrison, if you're not cheating on a spouse, and you didn't secretly video what we did, then I think I'll be able to cope." So long as it wasn't *actually* something even more terrible than that.

"It's about the power." He was grinning now, clearly unable to keep his face straight, and she was starting to get suspicious.

"What about the power?" she asked.

Harrison looked guilty. A cat-caught-with-feathers-in-his-mouth kind of guilty.

"Well, I wasn't lying when I said the power had gone out. That a fuse had blown. We both heard it blow."

She pushed back from him, holding the blanket tight to her and glaring at him. He was grinning again, so she knew it wasn't something hideous, but the look on his face...

"Harrison?"

"The power goes out here all the time, usually over winter, so we have a backup generator."

"So let me get this straight," she said, shaking her head.

He laughed and interrupted her. "I'm not going to lie. I could have flicked one switch and fired up the generator and we would have had power in the house almost instantly," he admitted.

"Harrison! You purposefully left me in the dark and then pretended we were stranded so you could, what? *Seduce* me?"

He reached out to touch her face, but she playfully slapped his hand away.

"Sweetheart, I'm just a bloke. I had a beautiful woman in my house, an excuse to keep the lights out..."

"I can't believe you did that to me," she exclaimed, trying hard to sound angry and completely failing.

"Oh, but you can," he said, refusing to let her get away this time, holding her wrists locked in place against his chest.

"Harrison," she warned.

"What?" he whispered, his voice silky and seductive.

Poppy just shut her eyes and let him kiss her. So he'd lied about the lights. So what? It wasn't like he'd had to force her into anything. And this Harrison, the laid-back version of him, she was liking a lot.

* * *

Harrison stood under the water, eyes shut as it hit his face. It was hot, almost to the point of burning, and he didn't want to get out. Maybe he should have asked Poppy to join him....

He stepped back and blinked the water from his eyes. What had happened last night had been fantastic, exactly what he'd needed, but he was starting to think it might have been a mistake. A good one, but a mistake nonetheless.

But if it was a mistake, then why was he thinking about calling her in to get naked under the water with him?

Harrison submerged his face again, trying to clear his head. It was just one night; one crazy, heat-of-the-moment kind of night that didn't have to happen again. *Unless he wanted it to.*

"Harrison, ready when you are!"

He held his breath for as long as possible before turning off the faucet. There was a part of him that wished what had happened could turn into something more, that it wasn't just a fun, one-night thing. *A big part of him.*

The truth was, Poppy was a great girl, and if he'd met her ten years ago he might have thought she was *the one*. But his wife *had* left him, he *was* divorced and he had two children who meant the world to him. Not to mention the vow he'd made not to let them or himself get hurt again, if it was at all within his power.

Poppy might stick it out, or she could stay a week or a month or two, then head back to her old life. Nothing was keeping her here other than her desire for a fresh chance and to feel she'd made a difference.

"Harrison?"

Her voice was closer this time, as if she'd come looking for him. He dried himself, then slung the towel around his waist and knotted it.

"Oh, sorry." Poppy stood in the open doorway, eyes downcast, cheeks pink.

Her shyness struck him, made him forget all about his rationale and think only about her.

"After everything we did last night, *now* you're shy?"

She laughed, but she was still avoiding him, even though they'd been naked under a blanket less than thirty minutes earlier.

"I don't exactly do this kind of thing," she told him, folding her arms across her chest and bravely staring back at him.

"What do you mean by *this*?" he teased, unable to stop himself.

"You know what? How about you get dressed and I'll see you in the kitchen for breakfast?" Poppy said, starting to back away.

Harrison had hold of her arm in less than a second, his fingers closing around her biceps. She didn't turn, but stayed dead still.

"You," he said, scooping the hair from her neck so he could breathe on her skin, run his lips across her warm flesh, "are doing something to me." Harrison stood close to her, his front pressed to her back, fitting against her. "And I don't know how or why, but I feel like every time I try to hold back, you reel me in."

"Really?" she whispered.

"Really," he replied. "Like witchcraft."

Poppy chuckled and spun on the spot, looping her arms around his neck and leaning back slightly. "Funny, but I feel like you're doing the exact same thing to me."

Harrison shut his eyes when she kissed him, wishing he was stronger.

"You do realize I have animals to check and feed?" he asked, rocking back to put some distance between them.

"Let's have breakfast and then you can show me how I can help," Poppy offered. "Deal?"

"You're actually going to come outside and try to help me?"

She shrugged. "Why not? I'm not some city princess. I just need to be told what to do."

Harrison shook his head. "Deal, then," he agreed.

Poppy grinned at him over her shoulder before disappearing, leaving him half-naked, staring after her.

Déjà vu. That's what it felt like to him. Because one day his wife had said the same thing, been so eager to see what living on a remote ranch was like. Then out of the blue she'd blamed exactly that in the note she'd left him, before running out on him and their children in the middle of the night and never coming back.

Poppy was so different, though. A kind, loving person he could never imagine behaving that way, let alone walking out on children. But he'd never thought his wife would, either. Which meant he couldn't read women as well as he'd once liked to think he could. And what if he made the wrong call again? It wasn't worth it. Not to him. Not to Katie. And not to Alex.

He needed to talk to Poppy, burst the fun, carefree bubble they had been living in since he'd rescued her from the river the night before. He didn't want to hurt her any more than he wanted to hurt himself, and the longer he let himself behave like this the harder it would be to walk away.

Poppy cleared the plates from the table and put the maple syrup back in the fridge.

"You know, you half deserved to lose everything in your freezer for playing that trick on me last night," she told him. It wasn't like she hadn't enjoyed herself, but still. She didn't like that he'd tricked her, or that she'd so blatantly fallen for it.

"I already had that one sussed out," he said with a grin. "So long as you don't open them, freezers are good for at least twelve hours with no power. I had all my bases covered."

He thought he was so clever. Poppy gave him what she hoped was a withering look. "So how about these animals? You still game for showing me the ropes?"

Harrison was giving her a weird look, one she couldn't read. "Am *I* game?" he asked. "I thought you were just saying that to be polite."

She laughed. "Would it surprise you that much to know that I actually *want* to learn? I'm part of a rural community now, so I can't exactly have the children I'm teaching know more about ranch work than their teacher, can I?"

"All righty, then." He stood up and stretched, looking her up and down. "But you do realize you'll need to wear something more…" he paused "…*appropriate* than that, right?"

If he was trying to intimidate her or put her off, then she wasn't going to take the bait. Poppy walked up close to him, standing in his space, eyes never leaving his. He wanted to intimidate her? Then she'd do the same straight back at him.

"Let's go saddle up, cowboy," she said, in her impersonation of a drawl.

His face showed no expression, but his eyes were glinting, and she knew he was trying hard not to smile. Harrison bent slowly, teasingly, and pressed a barely there kiss to her lips. "You have no idea what you're getting yourself into," he whispered.

"Try me."

He stayed in place, hands moving gently up and down her arms, before he backed away. "I'm not intentionally being hard on you," he said. "Well, I guess I am, but it's only because I don't think you should try to change who you are."

Her eyebrows rose in question. "I'm not trying to change who I am, Harrison. Is that honestly what you think?"

He shrugged. She could tell he was uncomfortable, from the way he was standing to the look on his face.

"I came here because I wanted to, Harrison. I came because I wanted a new beginning, and if the people of Bellaroo are prepared to give me that, then I'm prepared to push a little out of my comfort zone to embrace life here."

"I'm sorry." He was staring out the window as if he was a million miles away, even though he'd just apologized.

Poppy stayed by the table, not sure what was happening and wishing they could go back to how things had been a few moments earlier. When they'd been having fun and pretending they were both just two people with no issues and no ugly pasts to ruin their chances at anything great happening between them.

"I thought we'd already had this conversation," she said, her voice so low she was almost surprised he heard it. "I'm not *her,* Harrison."

"Don't you think I know that?" His own voice was louder than usual, pained in a way she'd never heard it. She'd seen him sad and stressed—when he'd been rushing to visit his dad in hospital and fearing the worst— but this was different. Now he looked tortured, as if he was struggling hard to fight his inner demons and didn't know how to stop them from haunting him. "You are *nothing* like her, Poppy. Nothing at all like her. But having you here, having a woman in my home after so long being on my own..."

Poppy crossed the room, touched Harrison's elbow and propelled him forward.

"Let's go outside and just enjoy hanging out. It doesn't have to mean anything more than you showing me around, okay?"

He nodded, but the anger and pain were still there— in his eyes and written all over his face.

"Yeah, you're right," he said.

Poppy looped her arm around his waist and gave him a squeeze. Maybe she should have been angry with him, should have told him at length how wrong he was about her. But Harrison wasn't trying to offend her or hurt her. He was trying to stop from hurting himself, and she understood that more than anyone else in the world right now.

"Harrison, you forgot about your dogs! Why weren't they crying at the door to come in?" Poppy dropped and gave the big dog a cuddle, arms around him. The other one held back a little, but she coaxed him over.

"My dogs are pretty lucky, Poppy. They don't get locked in kennels, they're well fed and they get treated well. And last night they were up at the worker's house, so they've only been down here waiting since this morning."

She shook her head. "They should have been inside, in front of the fire."

Harrison ran a hand through his hair before pulling on his boots and reaching for a jacket. "I'm already called the soft rancher by most of the men around here, so I think I'll pass on pampering the dogs."

"You're considered soft because you feed your working dogs properly and treat them with the respect they deserve?"

He laughed and this time it hit his eyes, making them shine the way they usually did. "They call me soft because I have an old sofa at the back door for my dogs and because I let my daughter convince me not to send a bunch of cattle she's fallen in love with to the slaughterhouse. So, yeah, that's considered pretty pathetic around these parts."

Poppy completely disagreed, but at least they'd moved on to a new discussion.

"Okay, what do I wear?" she asked, giving the dogs one last pat each.

"Anything you like, just take your pick."

Poppy liked looking nice, but contrary to what Harrison thought, she couldn't care less about throwing some boots and a warm top on, even if the latter was five times too big for her.

"Ready when you are," she said, grabbing the closest jacket and zipping it up. "Let's go."

Harrison was starting to see a pattern where Poppy was concerned, and he didn't like it. Not one bit. He hated being rude to her, acting as if she was somehow deserving of the stupid comments that he just couldn't seem to hold back, but she wasn't. Which meant he had to learn how to hold his tongue, get used to the hurt look on her face when he offended her or stay the hell away.

He clenched his fists. The last one wasn't something he wanted to do, but he knew it was the logical choice.

"Do we go through here?" Poppy was striding on ahead of him, hand poised on the latch to the gate.

"No!" he yelled. Harrison sprinted the short distance and slammed his hand over hers. "No," he said, more softly this time.

Poppy was frozen, her body like stone, and he gently lifted her hand from the gate.

"I didn't mean to hurt you."

"I'm fine," she mumbled.

He could see how strained her face was, as if he'd finally managed to push her that one step too far. Only this time his rudeness had been warranted.

"I have our stud bull in this field," he explained, pointing him out. Poppy followed his gaze, and he placed his hand on her shoulder, trying to reassure her, show that he actually did care. "The fences are all electric, but if you'd gone through that gate…" He blew out a breath. "On second thought, let's not even think about it."

Poppy was slowly starting to nod. "So you kind of saved me, huh?"

He grinned, could see she was seeing how amusing the situation was. "Yeah, I guess I kind of did."

"Maybe I should let you lead the way. You know, so I don't make some massive blunder that ends up with you needing to resuscitate me."

Harrison slowly removed his hand and started to walk again. Him having to resuscitate her was not something he needed to be thinking about, not with the thoughts of Poppy in his arms the night before still playing through his head like a movie stuck on repeat.

"Let's go through here. We can check on Katie's herd, walk down to the river and see how high it is."

"This might be a silly question, but don't you have hundreds of cattle that need to be checked?"

"I do, but with the size of this place we let the cattle do their own thing because they're on massive blocks rather than just in fields. They have hectares and hectares to roam, so we make sure they're okay, but in general they're just left to do what cows do." Harrison glanced at Poppy, made sure she wasn't bored to tears. "We do our mustering with helicopters these days, and I have a few guys working here full-time, so they'll be out doing the grunt work for me already."

"You love it here, don't you?"

Poppy's question made him turn. "What made you say that?"

"It's true, isn't it? I can see it in your eyes and the way you talk about the place. I don't even think you're aware of how your face lights up when you're looking at the land."

Harrison dropped to his haunches, scratching one of his dogs on the head. "That's why I'm so protective," he said, knowing he had to be honest right now, that he needed to answer more than just the question she'd asked. "I love Bellaroo Creek more than anything because it's the land I grew up on, and it's the land I want my children to grow up on."

Poppy's face was soft, her eyes locked on his, tears glistening. "I understand, Harrison. Not because I have a ranch or get your connection with the land, but because I know what it's like to have the home you love and the people you love snatched away without having any control over it happening or not."

He tried to smile and failed. "I need you to know that the Harrison you met that first day at school, that's not who I am. But the idea of having to sell this place and move to stay near my kids, to keep them out of boarding school..." He shook his head. "It's eating me up, one day at a time. It's all I think about, why I'm so sure you'll bolt and leave us. Because someone like you coming here and sticking it out just seems too good to be true."

He wanted to touch her, to connect with her physically and show her that he did care about her. That he wanted to think she *would* stay, but that he couldn't let himself believe it.

"Harrison, I'm not going to let this community down. Not if I can help it."

He didn't doubt her intentions, but past experience told him he wasn't always the best judge of character. "Poppy, what happened last night was great." He shut his eyes for a beat, trying to get his head straight, wanting to say this right.

"Geez, Harrison, I feel like you're breaking up with me."

She was trying to be lighthearted, but he could see she was hurting, and he hated being the cause of that. He'd already attempted to have this conversation last time they'd kissed, and now...now it was much more than just a kiss.

"When I met my ex-wife, I thought I'd met the person I'd spend the rest of my life with," he told her, speaking as honestly as he could. "When we moved here, she said she'd do it for me, that she wanted to give our life here a chance, and when we had Katie and then Alex, I thought everything was going great."

"So what happened?" Poppy asked.

Harrison leaned against the timber fence and looked up at the sky. "I knew she was struggling, but there was nothing more I could do for her." He recalled the day when he'd woken to find her gone and the reality of raising two kids on his own had set in. "When she left, it was so final. A note on the kitchen table, the car and some of her things gone, and that was it. For a while I thought she'd come back, that there was no way a mom could leave her children, but it never happened. And then I became so angry, so furious about the way she'd left and what it had done to my kids, especially to Katie at the time, and I couldn't see past it."

"But you did, you must have," Poppy said. "If you were that filled with anger still, then you wouldn't be the father I've witnessed firsthand with his kids."

Harrison nodded. "Yeah, that's true, but the anger is still there somewhere. It's never really left." He took a deep breath. "I mean, I can see now that maybe she wasn't cut out for motherhood or living here, but it still hurts me to see my kids grow up without a mom. I would do anything for my children, *anything* to protect them, and keeping our family unit together and free of any more pain is the most important thing in the world to me."

Poppy had tears in her eyes now. "And it's why you'd sacrifice your family's land to move away with them if they had to change schools. Why you'd give up what you love."

"Without a moment's hesitation."

CHAPTER THIRTEEN

HARRISON FELT AS if he'd been broken all over again, dredging up the past and reliving it.

"Do you know what it's like, to hold your baby in your arms, to look into his eyes and whisper to him that his mommy has gone, that she's never coming back?" Harrison choked, emotion ripping his throat and making him so angry he could have bellowed like a bear. "What it's like to want to do everything in your power to love and protect this little child when you have *no idea* where to even start? How to do it on your own? Not to mention having a heartbroken little girl sobbing in your bed night after night?"

He stared into Poppy's eyes and then wished he hadn't, because he could see how his words were hurting her, as if he was accusing *her* of something that she most certainly wasn't guilty of. But now that he'd started, he couldn't stop. He'd kept his feelings bottled up inside for years, locked it all away, and now that he was talking about it, everything was crashing back. The way it had been at the time, alone with two children, thrust full-time into solo parenthood.

"When you have a child, all you want is to give them everything. But there were so many times, late at night, when I'd only just managed to get Alex back down after walking him around the house for what felt like hours, then would get into bed and have Katie crying for her mom, that I almost gave up. Thought I couldn't give them what they deserved, the love they needed that only I could give."

Tears started streaming down his cheeks and he couldn't do anything to stop them. Because his children weren't here, he was talking about the past and he couldn't hold it back any longer.

"I had to be everything for those kids, two parents rolled into one, and it made me like a protective papa bear. And it's why I'll never be able to let anyone close to me or them again." Harrison wiped at his eyes, furious with himself for breaking down since he was usually so good at keeping his composure. "They mean everything to me, Poppy, and I'm all they've got. And while they're little…" he paused and stared out at the field, the young cattle Katie loved so much putting a smile on his face "…then I'm going to make sure I protect them the only way I know how."

Poppy had started to walk away. Harrison rubbed the back of his hands over his eyes and down his cheeks, refusing to let his emotions take over again. "I'm sorry, I don't know where that all came from."

She didn't stop, so he jogged to keep up with her, touched her elbow to make her halt. When she didn't turn, kept her face down, he stepped around her to force her to stop moving or crash into him.

"Hey, I'm sorry." Why the hell had he gone off the handle like that? Acted as if it was somehow her fault, that he had a right to just burst out with something he'd been sitting on for five years? Poppy hadn't deserved it, not when she'd been there for him this past week more than anyone else in his life. "Poppy, honestly, I don't know where all that came from, why I…" *Crap.* She was crying.

When he reached for her arm, she just shook her head, but he wasn't going to give up. Why the hell did he have to go and ruin everything? Upset the one person who deserved more than anyone *not* to be hurt?

"Poppy?" Harrison tucked his fingers under her chin, gently lifted until her eyes met his. They were swimming with tears, tears that hit him so hard because it was his fault she was crying.

"You're right, I don't know what it's like to hold my own child," she said, her voice cracking even though he could see how hard she was trying to be brave.

"I didn't mean it like that, Poppy. It's just that I've been sitting on all that crap, the past, for so long, and it just came spewing out of me."

She was looking out into the distance now, but her eyes found his again before she spoke. "Something I do know, though," she told him, wrapping her arms around herself, "is what it's like to want a child so badly only to lose it. To be pregnant and so excited, then find out you've lost that baby you've been so desperate to have."

Double crap. How the hell had he screwed up to such an extent, talking as he had without even thinking that

Poppy might have been through a tragedy of her own? "You lost a child?"

"I've miscarried twice in the past couple of years, but then, I guess, given everything that happened, some people might call it a blessing." She cleared her throat. "The last one happened not long before I moved here, most likely from the stress of everything, because aside from what I was going through, I'm as healthy as can be."

Harrison frowned.

"My wife said she wanted children, Poppy, but the way she left them tells me she didn't ever love them like I do." He was trying to say the right thing, make the situation better, but he felt he'd put his foot in it again.

"Just because your wife walked out and left your children doesn't mean every woman in the world would, Harrison. And it certainly doesn't mean that *I* would."

He groaned. "That's not what I meant. I know you wouldn't do that, Poppy. I was just ranting, saying things I should have talked about years ago instead of holding on to it for so long."

"I want a child more than anything in the world, Harrison. Children to care for and love, to be their everything, and I would never, ever walk away from them."

"I know that, Poppy. I don't believe you would."

"I get that you want to protect your kids, and I *know* that you're a great dad, but you need to stop looking at everyone like a potential threat." She'd blinked away her tears now, her strength growing as she spoke, her voice more confident than before. "Be careful, Harrison, but don't isolate your family so much that you find yourself completely alone. Because by then it'll be too late."

Harrison knew she was right. Every inch of his body, his mind, was screaming out to him that what she was saying was true. But he still couldn't admit it. If he did, it would be acknowledging that he'd been wrong all these years, that *he'd* been the one at fault.

"And what if you're right? That I'm wrong?" he asked, because he couldn't not.

Poppy touched his arm. "I know what it's like to lose something you love, and I know how hard it is to admit to being wrong. But you have to make up your own mind, Harrison. About what's right for you and for your family. Only you can do that."

"I know, but sometimes it's easier to push everyone away than take a chance on letting someone close." He swallowed, hard, and stared past her, because it was easier than meeting her gaze. Easier than acknowledging the truth of her words.

"Last night was great, Harrison, and I appreciate you showing me around this morning, but I think it's time I went home."

Crap, he'd pushed too far and said too much. He was usually guilty of the exact opposite, yet today he hadn't been able to hold back.

"You don't have to leave," he said, not ready to say goodbye to her, not yet. "I don't want you to think that…"

"What?" she asked, shaking her head. "That you have the same opinion of me as you have of your ex, just because I'm a woman? That no one else understands what it's like to have their heart ripped out by someone they loved and trusted more than anyone in the world?"

He shut his eyes, pushing back the anger so desperate to escape from within him. But this wasn't a fight he needed to have with Poppy. It wasn't her who had damaged him, who had left him, who had ripped his heart out and left him with two little children who'd become his entire world.

"I can't help the way I am, Poppy. Don't you think I'd do anything to wipe out the bitterness that's plagued me since she left? To take away the pain and protectiveness I feel for my kids?" He ran a hand through his hair, tugging at it, barely managing to keep the bite of fury back as it gnashed its teeth and threatened to emerge. "I don't *want* to be this person, Poppy, but I can't do anything about it. It's who I am and I have to deal with it."

She was the one angry now; he could see it in the flash of her eyes and the clench of her fists as she glared at him. "You're not the only person who's been hurt and left with a rough deal," she snapped. "Do you think I wanted to start over, to see everything I'd ever worked for snatched away from me? Do you have any idea what it took to come here to a new town, *alone*, and make a fresh start? With a stupid smile on my face, as if I was the happiest person in the world and not a woman who'd lost *everything*?"

"I know you've been hurt, Poppy," Harrison said in a low voice, trying his best to sound as sympathetic as he felt. "I'm not saying you've been hurt any less than I have, I'm just saying that this is the way I am. That

I can't get past what happened to me, what happened to my children."

"Try harder, Harrison," she said, her voice quiet but seething. *"Try harder."*

Poppy spun on her heel then, marching back in the direction of the house, and he let her go. Because what was he going to say to her?

Especially when the only words going through his head were too hard for him to admit to.

She's right.

He did a quick head count of the cattle and checked the fences, then walked up to the barn to get his quad bike. Climbing aboard, Harrison accelerated and headed toward the river, checking fences as he passed to make sure there hadn't been any major damage after the storm. He slowed as he neared the water, surveying its height.

Harrison turned the bike around and headed toward the house. There was no way anyone was going through that in a vehicle, which meant taking up the helicopter to get her safely over to her car. And after last night's experience, he wasn't sure she was going to like that idea at all.

He shut off the engine and went inside, taking off his jacket and walking in. Now he just needed to figure out what the hell to say to her.

CHAPTER FOURTEEN

Poppy stared into Katie's room. She hadn't walked in, but she couldn't move away from the door frame. It was girlie, but not over-the-top—pink walls so soft in color that they were almost white and pretty polka-dot curtains that reminded Poppy of her own room when she was a child.

It was the room she'd like to give her own daughter one day, but the thought of losing another baby still hit her with the force of a heavyweight punch. Finding out she was pregnant, *twice*, imagining holding her own child and then miscarrying. Her skin broke out in goose pimples as it always did when she thought about it. The rooms she'd planned, the tiny white clothes she'd bought as soon as she'd found out she was expecting…and here was a little girl with a pretty room and no mom. One day it would happen for Poppy, because it wasn't as if she couldn't get pregnant, but it seemed like a pipe dream right now.

She got why Harrison was so messed up about women because she couldn't imagine how any mother could walk out and leave two little children. But she hadn't deserved to hear all that. Not when she wanted to be a mom so badly, when she'd done nothing but be there for his children and for him. Not because she wanted anything or expected anything, but because she genuinely cared about every single child in her class that she taught each day, and because she cared about Harrison, too.

A tear escaped from the corner of her eye and she quickly brushed it away. She wasn't going to cry over a man. She wasn't even supposed to *be* with a man. So she most certainly wasn't going to blubber over this one.

"Poppy?"

She squared her shoulders and turned away, trying to forget the perfect room she'd just been staring into. Harrison was back, which meant it was time to go, and she didn't want to stay here a second longer than she had to.

The helicopter was hovering and Poppy was trying not to look down. They only had to go up and across the river, but after last night's experience she was still terrified.

They landed without so much as a bump, but her hands were shaking.

"Better than last night?"

Poppy glanced at Harrison and gave him a quick smile. She didn't want to be rude, but this was awkward and they both knew it.

She waited for his signal, not opening her door until he did his and keeping her head low just as he'd shown her the night before. Harrison ran around, grabbed her handbag and helped her down, but she kept her distance. She didn't want to look at him, touch him, *nothing*. Because then she'd only regret what had happened, the way she'd opened up to him and let herself just *be* with him. When she'd been scared and unsure, she'd pushed past it because it had seemed like the right thing to do. Because she'd trusted him. Now? Now she wasn't so sure.

"Poppy..."

She shook her head, more to tell herself no than him. "Harrison, don't. Please just...don't." As if this wasn't bad enough, standing here with him. The last thing she wanted was an apology or to talk about anything. All she wanted was to go home. To just get in her car and drive as far away from Harrison as possible. Because she should have known when they'd argued last night not to let things go so far between them.

"I just wanted to say I'm sorry."

He crossed the space between them so fast that she never saw it coming. One second he was passing her bag to her, the next he was grabbing her by the shoulders and kissing her so fiercely that she could hardly breathe.

Harrison's hands held her in place, his body solid like stone. She wanted to pull away but was powerless to, even though she knew it would be their last kiss. That she wasn't ever going to let herself be put in this position again.

He pressed his lips to hers over and over again, his touch desperate, as if he were a death-row inmate stealing the last kiss of his life. *With the woman he loved.*

Poppy pushed her hand between them, had to stop it

before it went any further, before she lost the strength to say no to him.

"Goodbye, Harrison," she said, her palm flat to his chest to keep him at arm's length.

Poppy turned her back and walked to her car, refusing to look over her shoulder. Her chest heaved, unshed tears, gulps of emotion tearing through her body. She fumbled in her bag for her keys, knowing that Harrison had to be staring after her still because she hadn't heard the helicopter fire into life yet. Could almost feel his eyes on her back, watching her leave.

Harrison was a good man—a strong human being and an amazing father, too. And that's why it hurt so much. Because the last man she'd been with had hurt her beyond belief, and in the end hadn't cared that she was leaving. Hadn't cared that he'd stolen all her money, that she'd lost their baby, *nothing*.

But Harrison? He was the exact opposite, and that's why he wouldn't let her close. That man loved his children so much that he would do anything to protect them, and was so guarded that he wouldn't take down his defenses for a moment.

Poppy started her car and tried to keep her eyes downcast, but she couldn't. Harrison was standing where she'd left him, his face unreadable, his mouth a grim line that she'd never forget. But he never took his eyes from hers, his gaze unwavering.

She turned the key, praying the engine would start, and then slowly pulled away and headed down the dirt road for home. In her rearview mirror she could see him walking away, turning his back and heading for his helicopter, but he was so blurred she wouldn't have recognized him had she not just seen him up close.

Tears fell in a steady stream now, curling down her cheeks and into her mouth, falling on her sweater. Poppy turned up the volume of the radio and tried to drown out the voice in her head telling her to turn around.

And the one telling her what a fool she'd been to ever let herself be intimate with him in the first place when she knew better than to fall for a man. Any man. Especially one as easy to fall for as Harrison Black.

Harrison waited for his children on the other side of the river, in the exact place he'd stood watching Poppy leave earlier in the day. A swirl of dust told him his mom was close, and the last thing he needed was her asking why he looked sullen. Telling her that the weather had gotten to him wasn't an excuse she'd buy, not for a second.

The car came into view then, and he fixed a smile and waved to the kids, knowing they'd be pressed to the window looking for him before he could see them. His mom flashed her lights and Harrison made his smile even wider, trying to convince himself that he was fine. That he'd had a pleasant morning instead of feeling as if he'd gone ten rounds in a boxing ring.

"Daddy!" The car door was flung open the moment the vehicle was stationary.

He bent down, arms out as Katie and Alex ran toward him. "Hey, guys." He was smothered in cuddles within seconds.

This was what he needed. Because this was what

he was trying so hard to protect, what he was giving up everything else for, to keep these little people safe.

"Hello, darling."

Harrison stood, one child in each arm. "Hey, Mom." He laughed. "I'd kiss you if I could."

She smiled back at him, shaking her head. "I was just telling your father that there probably isn't a dad in the world as loved as you are. Most kids like getting away from their parents for some fun, but these two just want to get back to Dad all the time."

He swallowed hard, refusing to acknowledge that one word—*parents*.

"It's good to know I'm wanted."

His mom sighed. "Darling, you're *wanted*. I don't think you need to worry about that."

Harrison wished he hadn't said it like that. "Dad okay today?"

She smiled. "He's spent most of the morning telling me he needed to come and help you."

Harrison put the children on the ground and watched as they ran to inspect the river. "Not too close," he called out.

When he turned back to his mom, she was staring straight at him, her mouth pursed as if she was trying to figure out whether to speak her mind or not.

"Just say it," he said.

She sighed. "You know I don't like interfering, Harrison, but the young lady who dropped the kids off last night seemed, well, lovely."

"She's just the kids' teacher." He *did not* want to discuss this with his mother.

"Sweetheart, she's more than just their new teacher. I can tell that from the look on your face, and it was written all over hers last night, too."

"I'm not talking about Poppy with you, Mom."

"And you don't have to." She touched his face, looking into his eyes so there was no escape. "But I've seen you struggle all these years, Harrison. I'm so proud of the dad you've become, but I know you could be an amazing husband to someone, too."

He took a deep breath to push away his anger, refusing to let his mom see him lose his cool. "I've already been a husband, and look how that worked out for me, huh?"

He turned to check on Katie and Alex, watching as they laughed and played together.

"I'm not saying you need to get married, but seeing you happy, seeing you spend some time with someone lovely who deserves your company, that would make me so happy."

Harrison swallowed his groan. "Point taken, Mom."

"You called her Poppy."

He raised an eyebrow. "So?" That was her name. What was so unusual about that?

"I was just wondering if the fact she stayed here last night was the reason you'd stopped calling her Ms. Carter?"

"How did you…?"

His mom was laughing. *The old fox.* Talk about cunning.

"I'm going to get these two back to the house," he

told her, leaning forward to drop a kiss on her forehead. "Thanks for looking after them."

"See you soon, sweetheart."

"Say goodbye to Grandma," he called to the kids.

They came running over to hug her goodbye while he watched. He'd all but admitted Poppy had stayed the night, which meant his mom would never give up until she knew more about their relationship.

Pity he'd made such a hash of things, because maybe his mother was right. Maybe he *did* spend too much time on his own.

"Is Poppy at the house?" Katie was looking up at him like an excited Labrador.

"No, sweetheart, she's home now."

"Did she stay in my room?"

Harrison held back a laugh. If only it was as uncomplicated as that. "Come on, let's get you two in the helicopter, okay?"

He lifted first Alex and then Katie, secured the door, then walked around to the other side. His kids had grown up around big machinery and helicopters, but they still grinned like crazy every time he took them up in the air.

"Copilots, prepare yourself for takeoff," he said through his mic.

The children were already wearing their headsets, seat belts done up and big smiles beaming at him.

Harrison took them up into the sky until they were well above the river. But he didn't want to go back to the house, to park the chopper just yet. He needed a release, a reason to remember why the land he worked was so important to him. Why he loved his life here, what he had to be grateful for.

"What do you think of a scenic flight around the ranch?"

The two happy faces peering out the window gave him his answer. They might not have a mom in their lives, but his kids were happy. They were loved and nurtured and growing up in an environment that most children could only dream of.

Maybe he was too hard on himself. Maybe he worried too much about what Katie and Alex *didn't have* instead of what they *did.*

Being up in the air was good for him. It was his addiction, and it had been far too long since he'd just enjoyed flying with his children by his side.

CHAPTER FIFTEEN

POPPY HELD THE envelope tightly and sat down. Her hands were shaking, unable to push beneath the seal to open it.

"Hey, Lucky," she said, watching the cat as he jumped up on the table and stared at her, his tail flicking back and forth as if he was equally anxious about the contents of her envelope. "What do you think?"

She hadn't been expecting it. That's what the problem was. What she'd been expecting was a pleasant trip to the store, trying to decide what she needed to buy for the week. Not Mrs. Jones telling her there was some mail for her, and getting *this* letter.

Poppy sighed and slapped the envelope down before picking it up again and sliding her nail through the seal. *She'd done it. Now she just had to read it.*

The paper was crisp, and there were a number of pages. The cover letter bore the emblem of a Sydney law firm, one she didn't recognize, and she had no idea how he'd even managed to pay for it.

Poppy glared at the page. Of course—he'd probably tricked his poor girlfriend into doing so, and she wouldn't realize she'd end up fleeced of everything she'd ever owned.

Poppy closed her eyes, took a deep breath, then slowly released it.

Chris in bed with her friend, her bank account at zero, credit card maxed out, her home up for mortgagee sale.

They were all thoughts she'd pushed away, refused to dwell on, but the memories were still there. Still so fresh and raw and painful when she let herself remember, still capable of sending a shivering shudder through her entire body.

Poppy opened her eyes and forced a smile. This could be what she'd been waiting for, the final piece of the puzzle she needed in order to move on with her life and leave those memories behind. Forever.

She was divorced.

She scanned the document over and over again, reading the words, studying the signatures.

She was divorced! She'd asked for a speedy dissolution of their marriage and it had actually gone through!

"Lucky, it's happened!" She jumped up and grabbed the cat, dancing around the room with him. "It's finally happened!"

The cat looked beyond alarmed, going rigid, but she didn't put him down. Because right now she needed a warm body pressed tightly to hers, needed someone to share the moment with. And if a cat was all she had, then a cat would do.

"Wine, that's what we need," she announced, heading for the fridge. "I want wine and I want it now."

Tonight she was going to celebrate. She wasn't going to think about her *ex*-husband, and she wasn't going to think about Harrison. All she needed to think about tonight was herself and what it meant to have a real fresh start, to forget she'd ever been married and just enjoy being Poppy Carter. Thank goodness she'd never changed her name.

Poppy unscrewed the bottle, poured herself a big glass and made for the living room. A night of wine, ice cream and *Sex and the City* was what she needed. Because after all this time, she was finally free.

And being alone had never felt so good.

Poppy held up the wine bottle and found it empty. She slumped back on the sofa and stared at her glass. Also empty.

She was starting to think that being alone wasn't so great, and seeing Big leave Carrie at the altar hadn't exactly made her feel great about herself. Unless she counted the cat curled up beside her.

A loud knock made the cat jump even higher than she did. Who the heck would be banging on her door at this time of the night? She stood and held on to the back of the sofa to gain her balance, not used to drinking so much alcohol. She usually stopped after her second glass, no matter what or where she was drinking.

Poppy headed to the kitchen first, grabbing a fry pan, then leaned against the wall as she walked to the door. The person knocked again, making her heart beat even faster. Who would hear her scream if she needed help?

She held the handle of the pan tighter, wishing she hadn't drunk so much.

"Who is it?" she called, her voice unsteady.

"Harrison."

Oh, dear. He was the last person she needed to see, but at least she knew he wasn't here to burgle her house or murder her.

"Just a minute." Poppy looked at herself in the hall mirror and almost burst into tears. Her hair was a mess, her mascara had smudged and she was dressed in a baggy sweater and ugly sweatpants.

She tugged her hair down and smoothed it, pulling it up into a more respectable ponytail.

"Poppy?"

She flicked the lock on the door and slowly opened it. "Hi."

Harrison stood in the half-light cast by the old cobweb-covered bulb hanging at the front door. His hair was messy, as if he'd been worrying it with his fingers, but his eyes were bright. They locked on hers the moment she looked at him.

"Coming here seemed like a really good idea when I left home," he said, shoving his hands into his pockets. "Now I'm starting to think I should have called first."

Poppy kept her hand against the door frame, steadying her body. "Are the children okay?"

He nodded. "Fine. They're asleep in the truck."

"Harrison, I need to tell you something—"

He interrupted her. "Me, too," he said. "Any chance I can go first?"

She held on tighter to the door, the lightness in her

head making her wonder if she was actually going to be able to stand and listen to him. "Ah, sure."

"It's just, well, I've had some time to think, and I feel like crap for the way I spoke to you earlier."

Poppy sucked her lip back between her teeth and stared at him. He wasn't exactly hard to look at, and she wasn't used to men apologizing to her.

"You were right about me being too scared to move on, that I needed to protect myself less and just, well, you know, you said the words."

"It's fine, Harrison. I know you've had a rough time, and you're a great dad."

"But that's just it, Poppy."

He stepped forward, into her space, his body too close to hers for comfort, or maybe just close enough. Harrison touched her cheek with such tenderness, such surprising softness, that she didn't know where to look or what to say. What he expected, if he expected anything at all.

"I don't just want to be a dad. I want to remember what it's like to be a man, too."

Shivers ran up and down her body, curling down her spine and across her belly. Was he talking about her, about last night, or had the wine just gone to her head?

"Harrison…"

He put his fingers over her mouth and the words died on her lips. "Let me finish," he whispered.

Poppy nodded. She wasn't capable of anything else, especially not with his hands on her, his body *way* too near.

"I want *you*, Poppy. I'm scared as hell, and I've

driven all the way here in the dark because I needed to tell you," he said, his voice so low she had to tilt her face up to hear him. "I don't want to think about the past or pretend like I know anything about you other than what you've shown me to be true. *I just want you.*"

He started to swim in front of her as if he was swaying, and she had to grip the timber frame harder.

"Are you okay?"

She shook her head. "No."

"I shouldn't have come here. I just, hell, I don't know what's happened to me, Poppy, but I can't stop thinking about you and I needed to tell you what was going on in my head."

"Harrison?"

He raised an eyebrow in question.

"It's not that I don't feel the same, but..."

"Was it something important you wanted to tell me? Sorry, Poppy, I just started talking and I couldn't stop. Do you have someone here?" He peered around her, as if he expected to find a visitor in the house.

"Two things, actually," she mumbled. "But no, no one's here except for me and Lucky."

He was waiting, silent as he watched her.

"I'm officially divorced," she announced, warmth touching her body as she said the words. "The papers arrived while I was at your place. I collected them earlier."

"That's a good thing, right?" he asked, a cautious look on his face.

"Yep, it's brilliant."

"What's the second thing?"

She laughed, unable to help herself. "I think I'm drunk."

Harrison checked the kids before jogging back to the house and taking Poppy's hand.

"Still sound asleep," he told her.

Poppy linked their fingers, but he pulled away in favor of wrapping an arm around her to steady her. She was a little wobbly on her feet.

"Do you want to carry them in?" she asked.

"No." Harrison steered her in the direction of her bedroom. "I'm going to put you to bed, then I'm getting straight back in that truck and driving back to the ranch."

If the water level hadn't retreated so fast he'd never have been able to visit her, and he didn't want an excuse to stay. Besides, he didn't trust himself around Poppy, and he didn't want to take advantage of an intoxicated woman.

He held her hand as she sat down on the bed, then bent to kiss her on the forehead, lips staying against her skin longer than he'd intended. But the truth was she smelled so good, *felt* so good, and moving away from her wasn't something that came naturally to him. No matter how much he'd tried to fight it before now.

"Did you mean what you said before?" she murmured.

Harrison knelt down on the floor in front of her, taking her hands from beside her and placing them on her lap, clasped in his. "Every word, Poppy. And if you don't remember them in the morning, I'm going to tell you all over again."

She was blushing, a warm red stain making its way up her neck and across her cheeks.

"I think I was a bit hard on you today," she said. "I mean, I was so annoyed with my ex, and when I got the divorce papers I wondered if maybe I was angry at you because I didn't want to be angry at him. So I didn't have to think about the past." She sighed. "I know, that doesn't even make sense, does it?"

He leaned forward, arms on her legs to steady himself. Harrison kissed her gently, softly touching his lips to hers. "I think we both need to forget about our pasts. Why hold on to something that could ruin everything in our future?"

He'd never found it easy to talk, especially about his feelings, but Poppy had done something to him. Had made him want to talk just to see the smile on her face.

"Does that mean we have a future?" she asked, her voice barely a whisper.

"Tomorrow," he said, kissing her one last time before standing up. "Our future starts tomorrow."

She smiled, lay back and pulled the covers up, snuggling beneath the quilt, eyes closing as soon as her head hit the pillow.

"I'll lock the door on my way out," he told her, bending one more time to touch her face, pressing his fingers against her cheek and then her hair before pulling the covers up a little higher.

Harrison made himself walk out. Reminded himself

that his kids were in the car. Because it would have been way too easy to lie beside Poppy and hold her, sleep beside her all night.

But he couldn't. Because if what he'd just told her was true, their future wasn't starting until tomorrow.

So he'd just have to wait until then.

CHAPTER SIXTEEN

POPPY SMILED AT the children as they laughed at her. She was reading aloud, the smaller kids tucked close to her feet, the older ones lying or sitting on the floor.

A tap at the door made her look up, book fallen to her lap. The door wasn't closed—she rarely pulled it shut—so she could see exactly who was waiting there. *Harrison.*

She'd wondered when she'd see him again, had been disappointed when he'd dropped Katie and Alex off and left in such a hurry earlier before she'd had time to say anything. To apologize for being tipsy when he'd visited; to try to figure out if she'd misheard her or if he'd meant it when he'd—

"Daddy!" Katie jumped up and ran to her father, giving him a hug around the legs before scooting back to her spot on the floor.

Poppy stood and held the book tightly in one hand, the other anxiously smoothing her hair back. "Hi."

He was standing in her classroom, or almost in it, as if waiting to be invited to enter.

"Sorry to interrupt, kids, but I need to talk to Ms. Carter."

She had to bite her lip to keep from smiling. When he said it all official like that... Poppy put the book on her desk and walked toward Harrison.

"I won't be a moment," he added.

She had no idea why he was here, but she wasn't going to tell him to come back later. She needed to hear what he had to say.

The smile he gave her was so genuine, so full of happiness that it took over his face, made his eyes crinkle at the corners and his dark brown irises even darker.

She grinned back, trying to stay nonchalant and failing. The butterflies fluttering in her stomach, as if caged and ready for release, wouldn't let her do anything different.

Harrison took his hand from behind his back and held out a bunch of flowers—wildflowers in bright purples and pinks. "I would have brought you roses, but it's a long drive to Sydney and back."

She laughed; it was impossible to do anything else. "You didn't steal these from anyone's garden for me, did you?" Poppy took them and dipped her nose into them, holding the modest bunch as if they were the most beautiful flowers she'd ever been given. And in a way, they were.

"I'll have you know I picked these myself, from my own garden, for you," he said in almost a whisper.

Poppy knew the children were listening, their ears all flapping like an elephant's, so keeping her voice low wasn't going to keep their conversation private. But talking quietly, intimately, felt right.

"Thank you," she said. "Nothing makes a girl feel more special than flowers."

Harrison stepped into her space, touched his fingers to her elbow in a caress that seemed more intimate than any she'd ever experienced before. It was as if a magnet was drawing them together, refusing to let them part until what needed to be said was said.

"Do you remember what I said last night?" he asked.

Poppy nodded. "I had a feeling it was a dream, but..."

"No," he said, shaking his head. "It wasn't a dream, Poppy. I meant every word, and I can honestly admit I've never felt the need to say something so badly that I've had to bundle my kids in a vehicle and drive in the dark because it couldn't wait until morning."

She held her breath, not wanting to believe the words he was saying. She'd been so deeply hurt by a man only months before, had felt so damaged and used at the time that she'd thought trusting another human being would be impossible for her. But Harrison... Right now she knew in her heart that she could trust him with her life.

Because Harrison was a protector, a man who would risk his life willingly to save those he loved. Would do anything for his children to make them happy, no matter what the sacrifice.

Her ex-husband... He'd been a taker, only she hadn't realized it until the bitter end.

"What does this mean?" she asked, not wanting to

believe what Harrison was hinting at until he spelled it out.

"What it means," he said, inching closer and taking her face into both of his hands, "is that I want to start a new chapter of my life. I want to trust again, and I want to love again."

Poppy swallowed, staring into his eyes, waiting for the words.

"And Poppy?" he whispered.

She nodded, hardly able to breathe.

"I want that person to be you."

She silently let out the breath she'd been holding, scared beyond belief, but happy, too. Exhilarated by his words.

"Are you sure we're ready?" she asked.

"All we can do is try," he said, his fingers brushing her skin while his palms rested against her cheeks. "I don't want to look back and wish I'd taken a chance with you, and know that the only reason I didn't was because I was scared."

"Okay," she murmured, nodding. "Okay."

"Yeah?" Harrison asked, his own voice a low whisper.

"Yeah," she whispered back, leaning into him as he bent down to her, mouth covering hers in such a gentle kiss she could feel only warmth as his lips brushed hers.

Poppy let him hold her, one arm tucking around her waist and drawing her in, the other still soft against her face.

A burst of giggles and laughter made her break the

kiss, but she couldn't bring herself to step from the circle of Harrison's arms.

"I think we have an audience," she told him, pressing her forehead to his for a moment before facing her pupils.

"Show's over, kids," Harrison said, blowing his daughter a kiss and giving his son a thumbs-up. "I'll come back for Ms. Carter after school."

She watched him go, laughed when he winked over his shoulder at her then picked up the book she'd been reading and settled back into her chair.

"Where were we?" she murmured, finding her place.

She had their attention on the story again, but hers was wavering. Because even as she started to read, trying to focus on each word on the page, all she could think about was Harrison. The man who'd just changed her world, her future, and was making her stomach flip as it hadn't in years.

Harrison stood outside the school, leaning on the bed of his truck, hand up to shield his eyes from the sun. He glanced at his watch. It was right on three o'clock, which meant he had a few minutes to wait before he knew how Poppy really felt about what he'd said.

And he'd never been more scared in his life.

Opening up to someone—putting everything on the line when he'd spent so long protecting himself and creating a safe little world for Katie and Alex—was terrifying. But he couldn't shield his kids all their lives. After talking to his mom, thinking about what Poppy had said…it had made him question everything.

Just because one woman, one cruel, heartless woman, had left them, didn't mean he had a right to punish everyone around him. *Especially someone like Poppy.*

He looked up as children's laughter and chatter filled the air around him. Poppy was walking behind them, like a mother duck herding her babies, and he stood dead still, didn't take his eyes from her. Her hair was loose and hanging down her back, her slender arms folded across her chest.

Parents were arriving, some walking and some by car, but Harrison didn't move. He wanted to watch the woman who had changed everything about his life, who'd made him change the way he thought and the way he wanted his future to be.

And if he had anything to do with it, she'd be the one to save their town, too. He wasn't going to let her go without a fight, and he wanted her to stay. Forever.

Harrison stood back, giving her space to take leave of all the children. His two came running toward him, jumping in the back of the truck.

"I'll just be a minute," he said, so distracted he wasn't even paying them the attention they were used to.

"Dad, that was kind of embarrassing before," Katie told him, leaning out the open window and flicking his back with her fingers.

"Why?" he asked, trying hard not to laugh. "Haven't your friends ever seen grown-ups kiss before?"

She giggled. "Yeah, but *you kissed our teacher.*"

He glanced in at Katie and Alex and they both smiled

back at him. He doubted they were that embarrassed, but he knew they'd want to know what was going on. They hardly ever asked about their mom anymore, but he knew a day would come when they'd want to know more about the woman who'd given birth to them. Even if right now she was just someone who sent money and a card each birthday.

The money he sent back, but the cards he read to them before tucking them away in a box beneath their beds, in case one day they wanted to read them again.

"Harrison."

Poppy said his name as a statement, not a question, but the shyness in her eyes told him she was as nervous as he was.

"I hope I didn't embarrass you before," he said, standing up straight and holding out his hands, palms up. "According to Katie it was all *very* embarrassing."

Poppy placed her hands in his, grinning up at him. She leaned in and stood on her tiptoes, her lips brushing his cheek in a gentle kiss.

"Kind of embarrassing," she said, her voice low, "but in a good way."

Harrison put his hands on her waist, staring into her eyes. He needed to know how she really felt, needed to know if he'd made a fool of himself to the one woman he'd opened up to.

"You're not going to abandon our school, are you?" Maybe he should have thought about that before he'd turned up and blurted out his declaration.

Poppy laughed. "You haven't scared me off, Harrison," she said. "I'm not going to run away with my tail between my legs just because you were honest with me."

"You're not?" He shuffled forward, holding her hands against his chest now.

"If anything, you've made me more sure about staying."

He raised an eyebrow, making her laugh again. "I have?"

"Yeah, you have," she whispered, standing on tiptoe once more and kissing him, smiling against his mouth.

"So you're going to save our town *and* me?" he asked.

"Yeah, I think I might just do that."

Harrison grabbed her around the waist and wrapped her in his arms, pulling her clean off the ground.

"How the hell did we find a teacher like you?"

She laughed and threw her head back. "Keep flattering me like that and I'll never leave."

He hoped so.

"So what would you say if I asked you to marry me?"

Poppy giggled like a child. "I'd say that I've only been divorced twenty-four hours and that you're moving a little too fast."

"Huh," he said, kissing her neck when she tipped her head back again. "How about moving in with me?"

"No," she replied, swatting him away. "But I *will* date you."

"Kids, we're going on a picnic," he called out, putting Poppy back on her feet and opening the door for her. "I think we'll get one of those cherry pies from the bakery."

"We are?" Poppy asked.

"We are," he said with a grin. "Because if you want to be courted, then we're having our first date right now."

EPILOGUE

POPPY STRETCHED OUT in the hammock, unsuccessfully stifling a yawn. The sun was just starting to disappear, but it was still more pleasant in the shade of the tree.

"Hey, gorgeous."

She looked up at Harrison's voice, pushing her hair back and searching for him. He was walking toward her, the kids running alongside to keep up with his long, loping stride.

"What are you guys doing?" she asked, sitting up and trying to get out of the hammock as gracefully as she could without tipping it.

The kids were giggling and grinning. Poppy narrowed her eyes and tried to look stern, knowing something was going on that they were in on.

"Why do you all look like you're up to something naughty?"

Harrison bent down and whispered something to the children, and they were practically wriggling on the spot now, smiles stretching their little faces.

"Harrison?" she asked. What was going on?

He started walking again, reaching out for her hand

and grinning at her. "There's something we'd like to ask you."

If they just wanted to ask her something, why were they all acting so strangely? "Okay."

"Poppy Carter," Harrison started, nodding to the children. They scurried up beside him, staring upward as if expecting to hear something so exciting they couldn't wait. "You're the best thing that's ever happened to us, and we want to tell you how much we love having you in our lives."

Tears welled up in her eyes, but she fought them, not wanting to ruin the moment. Because she might be special to them, but she couldn't even begin to describe how much they all meant to her. How much they'd changed *her* life.

She watched as Harrison nudged Katie. Poppy turned her face and smiled at the little girl.

"I love having you here because now it's like I have a mom," she said, her arm wrapped around her dad's leg, but her smile all for Poppy.

"And I love having you here because you bake yummy cakes and give me nice cuddles," Alex said, his voice a whisper.

Harrison cleared his throat and she looked at him, shaking her head. She knew he hadn't told them what to say, because it wasn't something he would do, which made it all the more special.

"I love having you here, too, Poppy," he told her. "There's nothing I don't like about having you in my life. In *our* lives."

She did cry then, couldn't stop the tears from falling

down her cheeks. "They're happy tears," she mumbled, wiping them away, not wanting the children to think she was sad. "It's just, well, I still can't believe that I'm here. With all of you."

Harrison squeezed her hands. She could see his eyes were glinting with unshed tears, too, and it wasn't something she was used to seeing. Her rugged rancher wasn't exactly the emotional type, so it hit her even harder, made her swallow an even bigger lump in her throat.

"Poppy, we have something we'd like to ask you."

She tilted her head, looking from Harrison to Katie and then to Alex.

"Poppy, I didn't want to rush things with us, but I know in my heart that you're the most amazing, kind, loving woman I'll ever meet," he told her.

"And we think you're the best mom we could ever have found, too," said Katie.

Poppy's heart had started to race. She could hardly breathe, her chest somehow constricting all the air in her lungs and holding it hostage. Surely he wasn't going to…

"So I'd like to ask for the honor of your hand in marriage," Harrison said, not even blinking, his eyes never leaving hers.

Katie was jumping up and down she was so excited, and prodding her brother.

"Oh, yeah," Alex said. "And we want to ask you to be our mom."

Poppy couldn't contain herself; she was so excited she thought she might burst.

"Yes," she said, throwing her arms around Harrison and kissing him, before tilting her head back and looking up at the sky. *Maybe someone up there did care about her, after all.* "Yes to being your wife," she told Harrison, before bending and opening her arms to Katie and Alex. "Yes to being your mom, too." They hugged her back, tightly. "I promise to love you forever and never, ever leave you." It was a big promise, but one she knew in her heart she'd be able to keep.

Harrison cleared his throat again, making her look up. He was holding something, waiting for her to stand up again.

She kept a hand on each child, but her eyes were for Harrison.

Oh, my goodness. He had the most beautiful ring in his open palm, sitting there glinting in the sunlight. A large solitaire diamond set on an intricate band.

"This was my grandmother's, and my mom has been holding it for years," he told her. "She has given it to me with her blessing, for me to give to you."

"Are you sure?" Poppy asked, letting Harrison slide it on to her finger.

"We want you as part of our family, Poppy. *For life.* So yes, I'm absolutely sure."

"I'm sure, too."

He took her into his arms, holding her carefully, as if she was the most precious thing in the world.

"We love you, Poppy, and we can make this work."

"I know," she whispered against his skin, loving his lips against her mouth, brushing her cheek when she pulled away.

"You saved our school, and you saved my life," Harrison said. "And I'll never take that for granted."

"You might have to find another teacher one day," she whispered, "because I think a place like this needs a big family, you know."

Harrison laughed, hoisting Katie and Alex up so they were all at eye level.

"I think you could be right," he said, stepping in so they could have a group hug.

Poppy closed her eyes and hugged her little family, knowing in her heart that she'd done the right thing. In coming to Bellaroo, in meeting Harrison—in everything.

This was her home now, and she couldn't have been happier.

"I just passed Sally and Rocky on my way here," Harrison told her. "I asked them to join us for a little celebration."

Poppy raised an eyebrow. The children were looking mischievous again. "Tell me what's going on," she insisted.

"Daddy said we're having a little party," said Katie with a giggle.

Poppy looked at Harrison and he just shrugged.

"You were that sure I'd say yes?" she teased.

Harrison put his kids down and grabbed Poppy instead, sweeping her up into his arms, dropping a quick kiss to her lips before carrying her inside, the children running beside them. "We have champagne and some treats from the bakery," he confessed. "Nothing fancy, but I thought you'd like to see Sally and have another squeeze of that baby girl."

Poppy couldn't exactly argue with that.

Seeing her new friend walking to the door, she wriggled until Harrison put her down. Once, she'd worried about being lonely in Bellaroo, but now she knew better.

"Hey, little one," Poppy cooed at baby Arinya. She gave Sally a hug. "Nice to see you, too."

The other woman grinned and gave her a hug back. "Are we celebrating?"

"We are." Poppy laughed and held out her left hand, showing off the ring on her finger.

She took Arinya to give her a cuddle and almost walked smack bang into Harrison.

Poppy met his gaze, felt the heat traveling from his eyes to her body. Next time it would be them with the newborn, would be them starting on the journey of parenting a new baby. But for now she just wanted to spend every minute with the family she already had.

* * * * *

Mills & Boon® Hardback
September 2013

ROMANCE

Challenging Dante	Lynne Graham
Captivated by Her Innocence	Kim Lawrence
Lost to the Desert Warrior	Sarah Morgan
His Unexpected Legacy	Chantelle Shaw
Never Say No to a Caffarelli	Melanie Milburne
His Ring Is Not Enough	Maisey Yates
A Reputation to Uphold	Victoria Parker
A Whisper of Disgrace	Sharon Kendrick
If You Can't Stand the Heat...	Joss Wood
Maid of Dishonour	Heidi Rice
Bound by a Baby	Kate Hardy
In the Line of Duty	Ami Weaver
Patchwork Family in the Outback	Soraya Lane
Stranded with the Tycoon	Sophie Pembroke
The Rebound Guy	Fiona Harper
Greek for Beginners	Jackie Braun
A Child to Heal Their Hearts	Dianne Drake
Sheltered by Her Top-Notch Boss	Joanna Neil

MEDICAL

The Wife He Never Forgot	Anne Fraser
The Lone Wolf's Craving	Tina Beckett
Re-awakening His Shy Nurse	Annie Claydon
Safe in His Hands	Amy Ruttan

0813 GEN STD HB

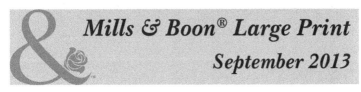

Mills & Boon® Large Print
September 2013

ROMANCE

HISTORICAL

MEDICAL

Mills & Boon® Hardback

October 2013

ROMANCE

The Greek's Marriage Bargain	Sharon Kendrick
An Enticing Debt to Pay	Annie West
The Playboy of Puerto Banús	Carol Marinelli
Marriage Made of Secrets	Maya Blake
Never Underestimate a Caffarelli	Melanie Milburne
The Divorce Party	Jennifer Hayward
A Hint of Scandal	Tara Pammi
A Façade to Shatter	Lynn Raye Harris
Whose Bed Is It Anyway?	Natalie Anderson
Last Groom Standing	Kimberly Lang
Single Dad's Christmas Miracle	Susan Meier
Snowbound with the Soldier	Jennifer Faye
The Redemption of Rico D'Angelo	Michelle Douglas
The Christmas Baby Surprise	Shirley Jump
Backstage with Her Ex	Louisa George
Blame It on the Champagne	Nina Harrington
Christmas Magic in Heatherdale	Abigail Gordon
The Motherhood Mix-Up	Jennifer Taylor

MEDICAL

Gold Coast Angels: A Doctor's Redemption	Marion Lennox
Gold Coast Angels: Two Tiny Heartbeats	Fiona McArthur
The Secret Between Them	Lucy Clark
Craving Her Rough Diamond Doc	Amalie Berlin

Mills & Boon® Large Print
October 2013

ROMANCE

The Sheikh's Prize	Lynne Graham
Forgiven but not Forgotten?	Abby Green
His Final Bargain	Melanie Milburne
A Throne for the Taking	Kate Walker
Diamond in the Desert	Susan Stephens
A Greek Escape	Elizabeth Power
Princess in the Iron Mask	Victoria Parker
The Man Behind the Pinstripes	Melissa McClone
Falling for the Rebel Falcon	Lucy Gordon
Too Close for Comfort	Heidi Rice
The First Crush Is the Deepest	Nina Harrington

HISTORICAL

Reforming the Viscount	Annie Burrows
A Reputation for Notoriety	Diane Gaston
The Substitute Countess	Lyn Stone
The Sword Dancer	Jeannie Lin
His Lady of Castlemora	Joanna Fulford

MEDICAL

NYC Angels: Unmasking Dr Serious	Laura Iding
NYC Angels: The Wallflower's Secret	Susan Carlisle
Cinderella of Harley Street	Anne Fraser
You, Me and a Family	Sue MacKay
Their Most Forbidden Fling	Melanie Milburne
The Last Doctor She Should Ever Date	Louisa George